*For Jennifer Hirsch,
with love and thanks*

Beforever™

The adventurous characters you'll meet in
the BeForever books will spark your curiosity
about the past, inspire you to find your voice
in the present, and excite you about your future.
You'll make friends with these girls as you share
their fun and their challenges. Like you, they are
bright and brave, imaginative and energetic,
creative and kind. Just as you are, they are
discovering what really matters: Helping others.
Being a true friend. Protecting the earth.
Standing up for what's right. Read their stories,
explore their worlds, join their adventures.
Your friendship with them will BeForever.

A Journey Begins

This book is about Maryellen, but it's also about a girl like you who travels back in time to Maryellen's world of the 1950s. You, the reader, get to decide what happens in the story. The choices you make will lead to different journeys and new discoveries.

When you reach a page in this book that asks you to make a decision, choose carefully. The decisions you make will lead to different endings. (Hint: Use a pencil to check off your choices. That way, you'll never read the same story twice.)

Want to try another ending? Go back to a choice point and find out what happens when you make different choices.

Before your journey ends, take a peek into the past, on page 182, to discover more about Maryellen's time.

Flying, that's what it feels like. My skis skim across the top of the snow so smoothly it's as if I'm a bird swooping low over the ground. I'm all by myself, with blue sky above, white snow below, and me in the middle, flying down the mountain, as fast as a shooting star.

I'm not skiing for fun; I'm skiing to win a race, and skiing to win is very, very serious. I'd love to go where I want to go, choosing whichever trail looks freshest and fastest and most fun. But I have to stick strictly to the planned race route and follow it exactly as it is marked and try to ski perfectly to win for my team.

It wasn't my idea to be on the ski team and turn skiing into something tense and competitive. It was my twin sister Emma's idea. She loves to compete. She especially loves to win. And she just about always wins when the two of us disagree. Emma is not only my twin sister, she is my best friend, and I always want to make her happy. That's how I ended up on the ski team. Emma really, really wanted us to do it together, so I gave in, as I usually do when Emma has her heart set on anything.

A sudden burst of wind makes the powdery snow

swirl up all around me. The sun reflecting off the snow blinds me just as the trail breaks into two narrow branches. I squint, looking for a route marker—a flag or an arrow—pointing to the branch that I should take. But if there is a marker, it's hidden by the whirling snow. Just then, someone waves, as if signaling me toward the left branch, so I take it. This branch of the trail winds through dense woods. Then, as I burst out into the open, it sends me over a huge mogul and I am airborne. That's fine with me. I love jumps—the higher, the better! But it's risky and unusual for a race route.

I zoom down the mountain, cross the finish line and pass the time clock, and—to my amazement—I win the race.

I'm happy, though not as crazy excited as Emma would be. Winning means more to her than it does to me. I take off my gloves, skis, and goggles, and change my boots. I put on my eyeglasses and look for Emma as I hurry to the ski-race awards platform.

"Good job, Sophie! Way to go!" cheer my teammates. They gather around me and thump me on the back. Even Coach Stanislav is smiling for a change. In

the crowd on the platform I see my proud parents and my grandmother. But where is Emma?

"Congratulations, Sophie," says the judge. She shakes my hand and gives me my prize.

"Whoa," I breathe. "Thanks." The prize is a fabulous vintage watch that's also a stopwatch. I take the beautiful watch out of its box, and I'm just strapping it onto my wrist when Emma appears.

"Sophie cheated," she says.

What?

"She took a shortcut," says Emma. "That's why she won."

"Emma, no!" I gasp. I plummet from happiness to humiliation in one second. How could she think that I would cheat? She's my sister, my other half, my twin. I know things have been a bit tense between us ever since our grandmother came to live with us and we've had to share a room. But is Emma so mad that she'd lie about me? Does she really think I cheated? I try to read Emma's face, but she won't meet my eye.

✻ Turn to page 4.

✻✻*✻✻*✻*✻*✻*

I 'm not quick with words the way Emma is, and now I struggle to explain. "I must have—I think I made a mistake," I sputter. "I was blinded by the sun, and I couldn't see any flag, and I thought someone pointed me down the trail, and—"

"Sophie!" Coach Stanislav interrupts. I'm not surprised; even to my own ears, my explanation sounds weak. "If you cheated," my coach continues, "just be honest about it."

"I *didn't* cheat," I insist. "I'd *never* cheat. It was an honest mistake."

My mom slips her arm around my shoulder to comfort me.

"We'll have to look into what happened, Coach," says the judge. She turns to me and holds out her hand for the watch.

I undo the wrist strap with trembling, clumsy fingers. By mistake I touch the stopwatch button, and—*swoosh!*

Just for a second—

Just for the blink of an eye—

Just like when I was skiing—I have the sensation of flying, like a shooting star. And when it stops, I find

myself . . . well, I'm not sure *where* I am.

I'm no longer on the ski mountain, that's for sure. Instead, I'm standing on a driveway by a small house. There's a station wagon in the driveway, along with a big silver camper trailer. A hot sun reflects off the trailer, and I realize that I'm roasting in my ski-team uniform.

The air is moist, and it smells nice, all fruity and flowery. The driveway is bordered with palm trees, flowers, and large bushes heavy with—*lemons*? I touch one. Yup, it's a lemon.

Where am I? What has happened to me? It's obvious that I'm not in my snow-dusted hometown of Cedar Top, North Carolina anymore.

I look at the watch, still in my hand. The last thing I did was accidentally press the stopwatch button. Could it possibly be the *watch* that transported me? If I press the button again, will it transport me home?

My heart quickens with hope. Maybe the watch will take me back to the moment on the trail before I chose the wrong route, before Emma's betrayal— before any of the bad stuff had happened yet.

But maybe the watch will transport me somewhere else entirely. Then what?

There's only one way to find out.

I touch the watch button, and . . .

Swoosh! . . . Once again, I feel as if I'm flying . . .

When I open my eyes, I'm back on the awards platform at the ski slope. Mom has her arm around me. Dad and Gran look sad. Coach Stanislav and the judge are frowning at me, and I can practically feel the chill waves of disapproval from all my teammates. It's as if *no time at all* has passed, as if no one has so much as taken a breath.

If only I could prove that I did not cheat, that I just made a mistake. But how? Emma, who usually leads the way and often speaks for me, is my *accuser.*

I feel lost, hopeless, and overwhelmed. Suddenly, I just want to disappear.

Will the watch transport me again? I'd like to go back to the warm place, but I'd rather go *anywhere* than stay here. I love the stars, the moon, and the planets—I'd gladly go to another planet right now!

No one will miss me; they are frozen in the

moment. And I need some time to figure out what to do about the ski race.

So, mustering all my bravery, I close my eyes and press the stopwatch button again.

✳✳ Turn to page 8.

woosh . . .

I'm swept up in the flying sensation . . . and when I open my eyes, I'm back on the driveway, next to the lemon bushes. I feel a warm rush of relief to be back in this balmy, palmy place.

I'm admiring the camper trailer—it's as stream-lined and silvery as a rocket ship—when the side door of the house opens and a girl about my age comes out.

She's skinny and cheerful-looking. Her reddish-gold hair is in a bouncy ponytail that catches the sunshine. A roly-poly dachshund waddles behind her as well as two cute little boys—one is wearing a fireman's hat—and a little girl wearing a tutu and a cardboard crown.

I freeze, expecting suspicious questions about who I am and what I'm doing in their driveway.

Instead, the ponytail girl smiles a friendly smile and says, "Oh, hi! I'm Maryellen Larkin! Don't you just love the Airstream trailer? Everybody does. By the way, this is my sister Beverly. She's seven. The fireman is Tom, he's five, and the littlest guy is Mikey, who's three. Our dog is Scooter. We're so glad you're here!"

The littlest boy, Mikey, runs forward and flings his arms around my legs, practically knocking my eyeglasses off in the exuberance of his welcome.

Maryellen rattles on. "We've been excited ever since we heard that you were coming. You're going to love Daytona Beach."

Daytona Beach? Isn't that in Florida? I'm in *Florida*? And Maryellen and her family have been *expecting* me? I'm so flabbergasted that I'm breathless.

Tom, the boy in the fireman hat, asks, "What's your name?"

"Sophie," I manage to choke out.

I don't know why, but my name makes all the Larkins smile. I've never thought of my name or myself as a reason to smile before. It feels good, I discover. I begin to relax a little.

"Sophie?" says Maryellen merrily. "Are you named after the singer Sophie Tucker? We see her on *The Ed Sullivan Show* a lot."

I shrug and grin. "I don't know," I say. I've never heard of Sophie Tucker or *The Ed Sullivan Show*. "Mom told me my grandmother thought up my name."

"My grandpop gave me the nickname Ellie," says

Maryellen. Then she asks, "How old are you?"

"Ten," I answer.

"Me too!" says Maryellen.

"Do you have any brothers or sisters?" asks Beverly-with-the-crown.

I nod. "A sister," I say, tensing up a bit when I think of Emma.

"Mom's excited to meet you," says Maryellen. "Your Aunt Betty is one of her oldest friends."

"Betty visited us last year," Beverly cuts in.

"It was Mom's idea for you to come stay with us while Betty helps your parents move from New York to Washington, D.C." Maryellen starts to lead me toward the house. "It's lucky that Betty works for the airlines, so your ticket was free. Let's go inside. Mom can call your parents and tell them you're here."

"Uh . . ." I begin. I'm so confused and not sure what to say.

Just as Maryellen starts to open the screen door, Beverly stops her.

"Wait, Ellie," she says. "How do you know that Sophie is Betty's niece? Maybe she's a new girl who's moving into the neighborhood." Beverly turns to me

and tilts her head. "Is that it?" she asks. "Are you and your family moving in?"

** *To go inside with Maryellen,*
turn to page 15.

** *To agree with Beverly,*
turn to page 17.

Carolyn plays a record on her turntable, "Rock Around the Clock" by Bill Haley and the Comets. My grandmother listens to the oldies station on the radio, so I recognize the song. But my grandmother wouldn't recognize *me* right now. Nobody would! I'm feeling so happy and free that I dance around all wild and rowdy with Maryellen and her sisters, belting out,

> *We're gonna rock around the clock tonight,*
> *We're gonna rock, rock, rock till the broad daylight,*
> *We're gonna rock, we're gonna rock*
> *Around the clock*
> *Tonight!*

We sing so enthusiastically that Scooter hides under a bed. Tom and Mikey come barreling in just as the song ends. When Mikey sees my watch, no longer covered up by my uniform's long sleeves, he shouts, "Tick-tock!"

Before I can yank my arm away, Mikey touches my watch, and—

Phew! Nothing happens. Apparently the watch

only works for me. It seems that I can "rock around the clock" with it, but no one else can.

"Mikey is crazy about watches," says Maryellen. "Once I cut a picture of a wristwatch out of a catalog for him and taped it on his wrist, and he wore it until it fell apart."

Mikey nods sadly and pats his wrist where his paper watch used to be. "All gone," he says.

You can say that again, Mikey, I think. If I clicked my watch I'd be "all gone" in a heartbeat. This is one tricky tick-tock!

I'm sorry that I have to be tricky, too. Part of me wishes that I could tell the whole truth about my watch—especially when Mikey turns his sweet, round face up and smiles at me. My heart lurches. I don't have any younger brothers or sisters. There's only Emma, who is one minute older than I am. The two of us look so alike that even our parents confuse us sometimes.

Once—before we understood how serious he is— we pulled a twin switcheroo on Coach Stanislav. It was Emma's idea, but I went along with it as usual. Emma and I are truly identical when we're both wearing

our ski-team uniforms, so one day, Emma wore my eyeglasses and we pretended to be each other. We were just joking, but Coach Stanislav got mad. He has always slightly distrusted us since then, so I've learned the cost of fooling people.

But part of me is afraid to tell Maryellen the truth: that I come from more than sixty years in the future. I'm afraid she won't believe me—and might even think I'm crazy and not want to be my friend.

** Turn to page 38.

I answer honestly. "No, I'm not moving into your neighborhood."

Maryellen smiles at me and says, "Let's go in."

I hesitate. Clearly, Maryellen thinks I'm someone I'm not. But Mikey takes matters into his own hands by putting one of his chubby little hands in mine and then pulling me toward the house. Fireman Tom shouts out, "Mom! The girl is here!"

Maryellen, Beverly, Scooter, and I follow the little boys. I notice that all the houses on the Larkins' street look alike, and they all look sort of old-fashioned. They look a lot like the house my grandmother used to live in before she moved in with us, and her house was built back in the 1950s. The Larkins must like that fifties style a lot—even their car looks like it's from that era!

"Your family's moving to Washington, D.C.," Maryellen says, sighing with envy. "You lucky duck. Have you ever been there?"

"No," I say.

"Me neither," says Maryellen. "But I love to travel, so I hope to go someday."

"*I* want to go to the White House," says Beverly

in a voice as queenly as her crown. "I want to meet President Eisenhower."

I get a funny feeling in the pit of my stomach. *Eisenhower?* Wasn't he the president of the United States a long time ago? Either Beverly is terribly mixed up, or something really, *really* strange is happening.

We go into the kitchen, and the funny feeling gets stronger. The appliances in the Larkins' kitchen look sort of—what's the word?—*retro*. The refrigerator has curved, streamlined edges and shiny silver trim, and the stove has big buttons and knobs. The wallpaper has roosters on it, and the curtains are flounced and polka-dotted. There's no microwave, no computers, no digital clocks.

Then I see a day-by-day wall calendar: It says that today is Tuesday, November 22, 1955.

∗∗ Turn to page 26.

∗∗∗∗✖∗∗∗∗

es . . . I'm new here," I say awkwardly.

"Well, welcome to the neighborhood," says Maryellen. "Where'd you move from?"

"Cedar Top, North Carolina."

"Cedar Top," sighs Maryellen, enchanted. "That sounds cool and piney and like it has mountains. Does it?" She doesn't give me a chance to answer, but says, "I'm always curious about places that I've never been, aren't you?"

"Well, yes," I begin.

But Maryellen rattles on. "Have you ever seen the ocean?"

"No," I admit. "North Carolina is a wide state, and I live way, way west of the ocean."

"The ocean's just two blocks from our house," says Maryellen. "Want to go see it right now?"

"Uh, sure, I guess so," I reply. I like Maryellen. She's so cheerful and curious, and I like the way she asks lots of friendly questions.

"I want to come, too!" announces Beverly.

"Me too!" says Tom, the one in the fireman's hat.

"Me!" says the littlest one, Mikey.

Scooter the dachshund tilts his head and barks, as if

to say that *he* wants to come, too.

"I didn't mean *everybody*," says Maryellen. "Just Sophie and me. You guys will slow us down."

"No, we won't," says Beverly. "You're going to have to stop off at Sophie's house first, anyway." Beverly's crown may be pretend but her queenliness is real as she says to me, "You'll need to change, Sophie. How come you're wearing a snowsuit?"

Maryellen, seeing me blush awkwardly, elbows Beverly and frowns at her for being rude.

"What?" Beverly whispers to Maryellen. "It *is* a snowsuit."

"Well, it's *cold* where Sophie comes from," says Maryellen. She turns to me. "I bet you have lots of snow in Cedar Top," she says enviously. "Last Christmas, I took the train to Georgia to visit my grandparents, and I saw snow for the first time. Don't you think snow is just *beautiful*?"

"Mmm," I say. Snow *is* beautiful, but right now the thought of it makes me shiver—not because snow is cold, but because it reminds me of the disastrous ski race. I push the thought from my mind, and answer Beverly's question. "I—um—don't have any other clothes here."

"Why not?" asks Beverly.

"Because they just moved here," Maryellen explains. "Probably their moving van hasn't come yet." Then she says to me, "It doesn't matter. You can borrow some of my clothes."

"Thanks," I say.

"I'm going to show Sophie the inside of the trailer, because I can tell she's dying to see it," Maryellen says to Beverly. "You go ask Mom if Sophie and I can go to the beach. And please get one of my dresses for Sophie to wear. She can change in the trailer."

"I'll go," says Beverly, "but I'm going to get something of Carolyn's. Sophie might be your same age, but she's bigger than you are, Ellie." This is true; you could practically make two Maryellens out of me.

Beverly trots off, and Maryellen explains, "Carolyn is our older sister. She's fifteen. She won't mind lending you an outfit. And we have another older sister, too. Her name is Joan and she's nineteen and she's married to Jerry and goes to college. I want to go to college and study art when I'm old enough. Do you want to go to college, too?"

"Yes," I tell her.

"What do you want to study?"

"Well, I really love the stars—" I begin.

"Oh, so do I!" says Maryellen. "Grace Kelly and Gary Cooper are my favorites!"

I laugh and shake my head. I've seen old movies with Grace Kelly and Gary Cooper, so I know who they are. "I like them, too. But I don't mean *movie* stars—I mean stars like in constellations."

"Oh," laughs Maryellen. She smacks her forehead as if she's waking up her brain. "You mean the kind that you look at with a telescope, not in a movie theater!"

"Yes. If I *had* a telescope, that is."

"How come you like stars so much?" Maryellen asks.

"Well," I say, "because they're pretty, the way they glitter. And I like the way the constellations have pictures and stories that go with them. You know, like one is Pegasus, the flying horse, and another is an archer with a bow and arrow. Sometimes I make up my own constellations and think up pictures and stories to go with them."

"That's neat," says Maryellen. "I like making up pictures, too."

I'm pleased. Emma's never once looked at the stars

with me. Maryellen's enthusiasm makes me feel as though *my* interest is interesting!

We go inside the trailer. Tom, Mikey, and Scooter follow us as Maryellen shows me around. The trailer is fantastic. It's a whole house with a kitchen and bathroom and bedroom and living room as tiny and tidy as the cabin of a boat.

We haven't been looking long when Beverly comes back and says importantly, "Mom says you can go to the beach but you have to take Tom and Mikey and me."

"Ohhh-kay," says Maryellen without much enthusiasm. She looks at me and asks in a soft voice, "Does your sister insist on doing everything that you want to do, like a copycat?"

"Well, no," I say. I always do what Emma wants to do, not the other way around.

"Lucky you. Beverly copies me," says Maryellen. "I complained to Mom, and she said that imitation is the sincerest form of flattery. But to me, it is the sincerest form of *annoying*."

For the first time ever, it dawns on me that maybe Emma doesn't want me to do everything that she does.

Wow. I never thought of it that way before. Does Emma
feel about me the way Maryellen feels about Beverly—
that I'm a pesky copycat trotting along in her shadow?
Maybe she'd be happier if I declared my independence.
And what about me? Would I be happier if I did things
on my own?

Beverly hands me a light cotton dress and some
sandals. "You can wear these," she says as if she is
bestowing a royal favor.

I hesitate. "Thank you—but this dress is so pretty!
I'd hate to mess it up. Maybe I should just borrow old
shorts and a T-shirt in case I have to wear them for the
next few days."

"But you can't wear shorts to school tomorrow!"
says Beverly. "Girls aren't allowed."

"Girls aren't allowed to wear shorts to school?"
I ask, surprised.

"Maybe it's different in Cedar Top," says Maryellen
apologetically. "But that's the rule here."

That's odd, I think. That's so old-fashioned. I look at
Maryellen's outfit, and then Beverly's, and I realize that
their outfits are old-fashioned, too. Maryellen is wearing a very cute vintage blouse trimmed with red

checks, and Beverly is wearing a dress with a sash and a full skirt that looks like the dresses my grandmother is wearing in all the photos taken of her when she was a girl, growing up in the 1950s.

Suddenly, a calendar on the wall in the trailer's kitchen catches my eye. It says November 1955.

That's when it hits me: The watch hasn't just brought me to Florida, it has taken me back in time more than sixty years!

I sort of stagger from the shock. Luckily, Maryellen shoos the little kids out of the trailer, saying, "All right, you guys. Let's give Sophie privacy while she changes her clothes."

Alone in the trailer, I plop down on a seat as my knees collapse beneath me. What on earth has happened to me? Why have I been transported back in time to this place, to this family? What should I do? I like Maryellen a lot; she is funny and friendly. And the little kids are cute. But should I *stay* here? I'm so sweaty with confusion and anxiety that I think I might melt, and my glasses are fogged. I take a deep breath. What always works best for me is taking things step by step. Maybe I can't solve the big mystery of why

I'm here, but I can take at least one practical step:
Obviously, the first thing to do is to change my clothes!

Oh, it feels good to peel off the hot, tight ski-team
uniform! I never did like it. It wasn't my choice; Emma
is the one who pushed for the sleek bodysuit so we'd
look as intense and serious as we're supposed to feel.
Now the idea of skiing makes me feel humiliated, sad,
and very confused. How could Emma say such an
awful thing about me? How could she even think that
I would cheat in a race?

It's true that sharing a room has made us tense.
Emma seems to hate everything I've moved into our
room, especially the glow-in-the-dark stars I put on the
ceiling. But it's not like Emma to be mean. She must
really believe that I *did* cheat—which makes me feel
even worse.

As I remove my uniform, it's as if I'm shedding an
unwanted skin along with Emma's terrible accusation.
I roll up the uniform into a ball as small as I can make
it. I want to drop-kick it into outer space, but instead,
I shove it into a closet in the trailer, shut the door
firmly, and turn my back on it. I like it here where no
one knows my shame. I open the door to the trailer and

step out into the balmy, breezy, sunny place that the watch has sent me to, feeling light and free, eager to see what Maryellen's world has in store for me.

When I emerge, the little boys and Maryellen burst out into applause. "Oh, you look so much more comfortable," says Maryellen cheerfully.

"You looked like a boiled hot dog before," says Beverly. Scooter barks in agreement.

Beverly's tactless, but she's right. "I *felt* like a boiled hot dog, too," I say with a grin. "Now I feel great. Shall we go to the beach?"

"You bet!" Maryellen says eagerly. "Let's go."

*** *Turn to page 31.*

*****✳*****

I gasp. What I'm thinking isn't possible: The watch has not only transported me to Florida—it has sent me back in time more than sixty years! How did this happen, and why did it happen to me? Weirdly, the date—November 1955—sounds familiar, but my brain is so fuzzy that I can't think why.

Before I can make sense of what's happened to me, Maryellen calls out, "Mom! Betty's niece is here!"

"Hello, dear!" says a smiling woman as she comes into the kitchen. Mrs. Larkin, who is wearing capri pants and sneakers, gives me a little hug. "Welcome! I was going to pick you up at the airport but your flight must have arrived early. Aren't you independent and enterprising to take a taxicab here all by yourself!"

I don't think anyone has ever complimented me for being "independent and enterprising" before. At home, Emma's the leader and I'm her follower. Although I'm still pretty puzzled as to what's going on, it feels good to be thought of as independent.

"Her name is Sophie," Beverly announces as she does a pirouette. Evidently Beverly is a queen *and* a ballerina.

"Sophie?" says Mrs. Larkin distractedly as she puts

Mikey in his high chair. "I thought Betty said your name was Cindy Lou. Oh, well, I must have misunderstood. I gave up trying to keep track of all my friends' children's names long ago." She smiles. "I can hardly keep my *own* children's names straight! This is Carolyn, by the way."

Carolyn, who's rolling up the cuffs of her blue jeans, looks like she's about fifteen. "Hi," she says. "It'll be fun having you visit. Since you and Ellie are the same age, it'll be like having twin sisters."

I smile and nod, trying not to flinch at the word *twin*, thinking of how stony Emma's face looked the last time I saw her. It takes me a second to realize that Carolyn is making a gentle joke. Maryellen and I don't look like we're the same age at all. In fact, next to Maryellen, I look like a giant Creature From Another Planet because I am so much taller and broader.

"We have another sister, too, but she's married," Maryellen says. "Her name is Joan, and she and her husband Jerry are students, so they live at the college."

"Oh," I say, feeling red-faced and sweaty. I don't know if it's from the heat or the confusion. Probably both.

Mrs. Larkin notices my discomfort. "Sophie, dear," she says kindly, "I know it was chilly when you left home, but you don't need that snowsuit down here. Why not change into something cooler?"

"I, uh, I don't have my clothes with me," I say.

Maryellen says, "You can borrow some play clothes from me!" She makes it sound as if I'd be doing her a favor.

"You can try some of mine, too," says Carolyn. "I think they'll fit you better."

"Carolyn is right," says Maryellen. "You're more long-legged than I am." She grins. "Lucky! I wish I were as tall as you!"

Long-legged? Lucky to be tall? I've always thought of myself as gawky, but now I stand up a little straighter.

"Come on," says Beverly regally. "Let's go to our room."

Scooter, who is far too fat and dignified to scoot, saunters behind us as we go through the living room, where there's a piano and a tiny TV in a giant cabinet. Tom and Mikey follow us until Maryellen shoos them off, saying, "Go away, you two!" She seems to think

they're pests, but I'm flattered by their interest in me. At home, Emma is usually the sun and I'm just the planet orbiting her.

The girls' room is small and crowded, but it's much tidier than you'd expect a room with three girls living in it to be. The shelves aren't overloaded and the closets aren't stuffed the way Emma's and mine are—especially now that we're squashed together in Emma's room since our grandmother moved into my old one.

Carolyn gives me shorts and a sleeveless blouse and sandals to change into. "Try these," she says.

"Thanks," I say. Carolyn's clothes feel deliciously light and loose after the tight, constricting ski-team uniform. The truth is, I've never liked the uniform. It's all part of how skiing got so serious when Emma and I joined the team this year and started skiing with Coach Stanislav, who is strict and demanding. When I peel off the uniform and put Carolyn's clothes on, I feel comfortable and, somehow, lighthearted. It's as if the heavy burden of my ski-team disgrace and the strain between Emma and me has been lifted, and I can float weightlessly, freed from gravity, as if I were in outer space.

"Oh, you look much more comfortable," says

Maryellen. "Carolyn's clothes fit you pretty well."

"Yes, they look good on you," says Queen Beverly, giving the royal stamp of approval.

"Do you like music?" asks Carolyn. I nod, and her eyes light up. "Do you like *rock 'n' roll*?" she asks in a conspiratorial whisper, as if rock 'n' roll is some sort of special secret.

I nod again, and Maryellen exclaims, "Just wait till you hear this record—it's our favorite!"

*** *Turn to page 12.*

G oing to the beach turns out to be more easily said than done. Tom has to be talked *out* of riding to the beach in his miniature fire engine. Mikey has to be talked *into* riding in his stroller. Beverly insists on adding to her outfit what she calls her "ballerina cape," which has ballet shoes embroidered on it. Scooter has fallen asleep and has to be awakened, which makes him snort a lot. I'm sort of chuckling, because the kids and Scooter seem comical to me, but I can tell that Maryellen is impatient. As she wheels her bike out of the carport, she mutters, "We'd be at the beach already if we didn't have these slowpokes tagging along."

When we finally have everyone ready to go, I'm the one who hesitates. "Don't we have to ask a grown-up to come with us?" I ask.

"No," says Maryellen. "As long as we're not going swimming."

How odd—in Maryellen's time, it seems people had strict rules about what you could wear to school, but a bunch of kids could go to the beach by themselves. I must say, it feels great to be so independent. And perfectly safe, too, because lots of people in Maryellen's

neighborhood are out on their front lawns or working in their gardens or washing their big, shiny cars
with tail fins and giant chrome bumpers. Everyone
is friendly, too. "Hi there, kids," says a woman as we
pass. She smiles at Maryellen. "Now, which Larkin are
you—Carolyn?"

"No, ma'am, I'm Maryellen," she says, sounding
polite but as if she has answered this same question a
million times. I know exactly how she feels; every day
of my life people ask me if I'm Emma. I guess kids in
big families are sometimes mistaken for one another,
just as twins are.

Maryellen introduces me. "This is my new friend,
Sophie."

"Nice to meet you, dear," says the woman. Then she
waves us off. "Have fun, kids."

I can see the ocean glinting in front of us, because
the street leads straight to it without a bend or curve.
The street is lined with tidy, matching houses, each
with a palm tree in the front yard.

"Does our neighborhood look boring to you?"
Maryellen asks. "I mean because all the houses are the
same. I tried to make our house stand out by painting

our front door red. But even the streets are flat and dull in our neighborhood."

"I like it," I say. For one thing, there cannot possibly be any skiing here! In Cedar Top, the roads are very hilly with lots of sharp and sudden twists. It makes me feel calm to walk on these broad, level streets. The air is soft and smells like oranges. The sky is blue and endless, and the flowers are bright. Even the cars are colorful; some are aqua, some are pink, and some are lemon yellow. I tell Maryellen, "It looks like paradise to me."

Paradise or not, Tom's had it with walking. "I'm tired," he says, plunking himself down on the curb. Scooter sits next to him.

"We're almost there," urges Maryellen.

Tom won't budge, and neither will Scooter. Sighing with exasperation, Maryellen picks up Scooter and puts him in the basket of her bike.

"Let's pretend we're in a parade," I say as I lift Tom and put him on my shoulders. "Beverly, you lead us. You're the drum majorette."

"The *ballerina queen* drum majorette," Beverly corrects me. She takes the lead and does balletic leaps along the sidewalk, her cape fluttering gracefully in the

balmy breeze. Maryellen is next, wheeling her bike with Scooter in the basket. And I am last, pushing Mikey in his stroller and carrying Tom on my shoulders.

Maryellen grins at me. "Thanks," she says. "You're a genius with little kids."

I grin and blush. That's kind of a nice surprise. No one has ever called me a genius with little kids before. Then again, I've never been around little kids, except for Daria, who comes with her mother, a secretarial assistant who has been helping my grandmother organize her books and belongings since she moved into our house. Emma and I studiously ignore Daria, who wrecked Emma's laptop the one time she came into our room. I wonder, would I be a genius with Daria if I tried?

Our parade reaches the beach in no time, and Tom wriggles to get down from my shoulders. He's not too tired to run on the sand! Maryellen lifts Scooter out of her bike basket and Mikey out of his stroller, and he and Scooter toddle and waddle, following Beverly, who pirouettes across the sand.

"Whoa," I say as I walk toward the water with Maryellen. We reach the edge and the waves lap our

feet. "I've never seen the ocean in real life before. It's really—big."

"You bet," says Maryellen. "Isn't it fantastic?"

"Mm-hmm," I say. The truth is, I'm overwhelmed by the crash and roar of the waves, the glare of the sun bouncing off the water, and the enormous, stretch-to-the-sky hugeness of it all. I'm glad that we're not allowed to swim. Standing at the edge is enough for me. I feel the tug of the water swirling around my legs, and the way the ebbing waves pull away the sand I'm standing on, and the hard pull of the undertow. I back up and stand safely away from the lapping waves next to Scooter, watching as Maryellen, Beverly, Tom, and Mikey race to the edge of the water and then race away, chased by the incoming waves, gleefully laughing all the while.

Maryellen beckons to me. "Come on, Sophie!" she calls. "It's fun."

I smile but shake my head. After racing a few more waves, Maryellen and her siblings come away from the water to join me. "What's the matter?" Maryellen asks.

I say shamefacedly, "I hate to admit it—I know

it's stupid—but I think I'm scared of the ocean. It's so *gigantic*."

Tom slips his hand into mine, Mikey pats my leg, and Scooter sits on my foot to comfort me.

"That's not stupid at all," says Maryellen earnestly. "It's smart to be a little scared of something as big as the ocean."

"Are *you* afraid of anything?" I ask Maryellen, as we start to walk home from the beach.

"Yes," says Maryellen gravely. "When I was little, I had polio. It hurt terribly, and even now that I'm better, one of my legs is weaker and sometimes I get out of breath."

"Are you scared your polio will come back?" I ask.

"Yes." Maryellen nods. "I'm also afraid that people will assume that I'm weak because I had polio." She looks fierce. "I hate that."

"And that's not the only thing you're afraid of, Ellie," Beverly pipes. She turns to me and says, "Ellie's scared of talking in front of people. You should have seen her at her birthday party. She wrote a show to raise money to fight polio, and we all had songs and dances and acts to do. Mine was the best; I was a

ballerina." Beverly does a plié on the sidewalk to demonstrate, and then goes on, "When it was Ellie's turn to speak, she just stood there like a statue."

"It's true," Maryellen admits. "I still get shaky thinking of it. I never thought that I'd be afraid of performing! I mean, I wrote the whole show! And I've always wanted to be on TV, for Pete's sake. But it turned out that standing in front of a live audience, with all those faces looking at me, made me freeze right up with stage fright."

"What happened?" I ask. "Did you get unfrozen?"

"Nope," says Maryellen.

"A terrible boy named Wayne did all the talking for her," says Beverly.

Maryellen shudders, remembering. "It was . . ."

"Embarrassing," says Beverly.

"Very," agrees Maryellen.

** Turn to page 45.

*****✲****

hen we go back into the kitchen, Mrs. Larkin says, "That's better, Sophie. Now you look cool and comfortable. This would be a good time to call your parents and let them know that you're here."

She points to a phone as big as a shoe box. I've never actually used a dial phone before, but I've seen people use them in old movies, so I know that you spin the dial with your fingertip. I'm pretty sure that I won't be able to call my parents on this phone or any phone. But I dial our number anyway. The line gets all crackly, and then goes dead. "I don't think I can call my parents," I say, truthfully. "The line is dead."

"They must have cut off their phone service now that they're on their way to Washington, D.C.," says Mrs. Larkin. "I'm sure they'll call us when they have their new phone number."

I don't have to say anything because just then Maryellen says, "Mom, can Sophie and I go outside?"

"You mean, *may* you go, and yes, you may," says Mrs. Larkin. "Come back when the streetlights go on, and we'll have dinner. Dad'll be home a little late."

"Okay, Mom!" says Maryellen. As we go outside, she says, "My friends and I usually play hide-and-seek

before dinner. Would you like to play?"

I nod. I've only ever played hide-and-seek indoors, so Maryellen's game sounds like fun.

"Olley-olley-in-come-free!" hollers Maryellen, and kids run over to the Larkins' front yard, coming out of other yards and houses.

I hang back, feeling shy, but Maryellen says, "Everybody, this is Sophie. Let's play hide-and-seek." And that's that. I'm part of the game.

Even though it's November, it feels like summer— not just because the weather is warm, but also because we seem to have all the time in the world to play. At home, Emma and I do homework before dinner if we're not at a club meeting or team practice. For us, every minute is scheduled and every activity is orga- nized and run by grown-ups. Here, some grown-ups are mowing lawns or chatting, so they're around if we need them. But they kind of just leave us alone. It's nice.

When the streetlights go on, Mrs. Larkin calls us for dinner. As we file in, she orders, "Wash your hands, please."

We do, and then we sit at a table in a little nook in the kitchen. Mrs. Larkin gently corrects Maryellen, who

is leaning on the table, by reciting,

> Mabel, Mabel, do be able.
> Take your elbows off the table.

We all giggle, but we also sit up very straight with our hands in our laps as Mrs. Larkin serves dinner. It's spaghetti and meatballs out of a can, with cheese to sprinkle on top.

"Thank you!" I say as Mrs. Larkin gives me a plate. "I love spaghetti, and at home we never have it with meatballs and cheese on top. My grandmother is a vegetarian, and my sister is lactose intolerant."

Everyone looks completely puzzled. Tom very kindly forks a meatball onto my plate, understanding only that I'm meatball deprived.

Mrs. Larkin says, "My! Well, I'm glad you like it." And everyone happily goes back to eating. Mrs. Larkin keeps a sharp eye on Mikey, who is determined to eat his spaghetti by the fistful. Scooter is keeping a sharp eye on Mikey, too. He slurps up noodles that slip out of Mikey's grasp and fall on the floor.

In the middle of dinner, Mr. Larkin comes home. He

reminds me of my dad: He's tall and cheery, with his suit jacket flung over his shoulder and the newspaper tucked under his arm. "Hi, kids!" he says.

"Hi, Dad!" they all say.

Mr. Larkin kisses Mrs. Larkin, then looks at me and says, "Hello there! Where did you come from? Did you drop from the sky?"

I know he's joking, but still I blush.

All the kids talk at once. They're loud, because it's hard to be heard in the tumult.

"She's Sophie, the girl we've been waiting for!"

"She's Betty's niece, remember?"

"Her family's moving to Washington, D.C."

"She came on a plane!"

"Tick-tock!" shouts Mikey, to be sure his dad notices my watch. Mikey doesn't know it, but he has come closest to the true explanation of how I got here.

"Well, welcome, Sophie. We've been expecting you. And thank goodness you've come," says Mr. Larkin. "It's been dull around here with only five children. Too quiet entirely. You're just what we need."

"Thank you," I say. He would be surprised if he knew how his words go straight to my heart. The

Larkins have a way of making me feel special just for being *me*. And they all have this "the more the merrier" attitude that makes me feel genuinely welcome. It crosses my mind that Emma and I certainly could have been more welcoming to my grandmother. She has tried to get to know us better, but we haven't responded.

As Mrs. Larkin bustles about fixing a plate for him, Mr. Larkin washes his hands. When he sits at the table, he says, "So, Sophie, you're going to be a Washingtonian, eh? That's good! You can keep an eye on how the government is doing up there. If you run into President George Washington, say hello for me."

We all laugh. "No, Dad!" says Beverly importantly. "George Washington isn't president anymore. Eisenhower is."

"Oh, right," says Mr. Larkin. "And the president lives in the Pink House."

"No, no," everyone laughs, delighted.

"Not pink. White," says Maryellen.

Mr. Larkin looks mischievous. He winks at me and says, "If our Ellie got her hands on that house, it would be pink."

Everyone bursts out laughing again. I look at
Maryellen for an explanation.

"I was trying to paint the front door red," she says.
"Your Aunt Betty was coming to visit, and I wanted to
impress her by making our house look different from
all the other houses."

"Ellie likes to stand out," says Carolyn fondly.

Maryellen goes on, "But I was wearing roller
skates, and Joan knocked me over, and red paint went
flying—"

"And it ruined Jerry's tennis whites, and the brown-
ies burned, and Mikey painted red stripes on Scooter,"
Beverly pipes up, "and Tom squirted the hose into the
kitchen and it was a terrible mess."

"And even after Ellie scrubbed and scrubbed, the
front porch was pink," says Carolyn.

"It still is," moans Maryellen, amid her family's
gales of laughter.

I join in, because I can see that Maryellen is not at
all embarrassed at how everyone is laughing at her
expense. In fact, she seems to *like* being the focus of
their attention and the reason for their laughter. Clearly,
Maryellen's family has forgiven Maryellen her mistake.

I wonder, will my family forgive me mine? Maryellen is laughing at her mistake. Will I ever be able to laugh at mine?

"But I *would* like to see the White House," says Maryellen earnestly, "and all the art museums in Washington. Can we go someday, Dad?"

Mr. and Mrs. Larkin exchange a look, and Mrs. Larkin says, "Yes, go ahead, darling, please. I can't keep the surprise a secret anymore!"

"Surprise?" say Beverly, Carolyn, and Maryellen all together. "What surprise?"

"We," announces Mr. Larkin, "are going on a trip."

✷✷ *Turn to page 47.*

When we get back to the Larkins' house, Maryellen brings me inside and introduces me to her mother. "Mom," she says, "this is Sophie. She's new here in the neighborhood."

"Welcome, Sophie!" says Mrs. Larkin. The way she says it and the warmth of her smile make me feel truly welcome. Mrs. Larkin is ironing the wrinkles out of a dress. She is wearing capri pants, a checked blouse, and a headscarf tied in a big bow, just like Lucy from *I Love Lucy*. Emma and I like to watch reruns of that show.

"Can Sophie stay for dinner?" Maryellen asks.

"Not *can*," corrects Mrs. Larkin. "*May* Sophie stay for dinner. And yes, of course she may."

"And *may* she spend the night?" asks Maryellen. "Tomorrow's only a half day since it's the day before Thanksgiving vacation. So can—*may* Sophie sleep over and go to school with me tomorrow morning?"

"Yes," says Mrs. Larkin. She smiles at me as she unplugs the iron and collapses the ironing board. "You had better call your family to be sure it's all right." She nods toward a wall phone that has a long cord hanging down like a tail. The cord connects the part you hold in your hand and talk into with the part on the wall

that has a circular dial on it. She turns to the rest of the
kids. "Come on, let's go wash your hands for dinner."

Everyone leaves, and I'm alone in the kitchen with
Scooter. Uh-oh. I stare at the telephone. Now what do
I do? When Maryellen comes back, should I tell her
that my family insists that I come home? I could say
good-bye and then click the watch and disappear from
Maryellen's life forever. But, oh, I don't want to! I like
it here. Besides, I'm not sure that I'm ready to go back
and face all those people who think I cheated. Maybe I
should just tell Maryellen that I have permission to stay
for dinner and spend the night. I don't need to explain
that I gave *myself* permission.

Either way, I'll have to be a phony phoner and pretend that I called home.

**** To go home,
     turn to page 51.**

**** To stay,
     turn to page 53.**

A trip?" repeats Maryellen. "I love to travel!"

"My old navy buddy, Dave Blanchard, has been asking to borrow the Airstream," says Mr. Larkin. "Guess where he lives? Washington, D.C."

"We figured we'd get around to bringing the Airstream to Dave eventually," says Mrs. Larkin. "But when Betty told us that Sophie was coming, we decided this was the perfect time to drive the trailer to Washington, D.C., because we could give Sophie a ride home. It'll be a surprise for her family."

"Sophie can use her return ticket another time," says Mr. Larkin. "We leave tomorrow!"

"Hurray!" everyone cheers.

Maryellen jumps up. "What a great idea!" she exclaims, hugging her dad and mom and then me. Carolyn and Beverly get up and dance, spinning and leaping around the kitchen, and Tom makes a sound like a siren to express his happiness. Mikey doesn't have a clue about why everyone is happy, but he bangs his spoon on the tray of his high chair all the same. Scooter barks on general principle.

"Joan and Jerry will stay at the house and take care of Scooter for us," says Mrs. Larkin. "The rest of us will

spend Thanksgiving with Grandmom and Grandpop in Georgia. Tom and Mikey will stay with them while we wend our way up to Washington, D.C."

"Grandmom and Grandpop!" the kids repeat joyously. They're clearly more excited about their grandparents than Emma and I are about our grandmother.

"We'll leave the trailer with Dave Blanchard, and he'll return it at Christmastime," says Mr. Larkin.

"But how will we get home?" asks Carolyn.

"We'll fly," says Mr. Larkin, looking excited.

"Fly?" shriek Beverly, Maryellen, and Carolyn. "We've never flown before."

"That way you kids won't miss much school," says Mrs. Larkin. "Only the day before Thanksgiving and the Monday and Tuesday after it."

"Oh, the Wednesday before Thanksgiving is only a half day, and we mostly just make turkeys out of pinecones and sing Thanksgiving songs anyway," says Maryellen breezily.

"Besides," says Carolyn, "it'll be a very educational trip. Washington, D.C. is our nation's capital. It's full of history."

"And art museums!" says Maryellen ecstatically.

"What do *you* think of our travel plans, Sophie?"

"Well . . ." I begin. I know that never in a million years would Emma and I skip school for a trip. We have so many tests and assignments and projects. And Coach Stanislav would pitch a fit if we skipped ski-team practice. At home, I always have a nervous voice inside me reminding me of Things I Have To Do. But the Larkins seem to do things just for the fun of it. So, even though it's not like shy and careful me, I hug Maryellen impulsively, and I say, "I think they're wonderful!"

"Hurray!" everyone cheers.

And what, asks that nervous voice inside me, *will you do when you get to Washington?* The happy attitude of the Larkins must be contagious because I reply to myself, *Oh, who knows? I guess we'll just see what happens when it happens!*

Of course, later, after we're all in bed and the lamps are out and the moon is pouring its light into the room, my worries pour in, too. Here I am, all snug in my bunk, listening to Scooter snore, surrounded by the Larkin sisters, who have been so kind to me. It makes me miss my sister Emma, who, up until this morning, was my best and closest friend. Shouldn't I go back and

straighten it all out with Emma about the ski race? My mother, father, and grandmother looked so sad. Don't I owe it to them to clear up this misunderstanding and fight the accusation that I am a—a cheater?

As I brood, I find that I have a lump in my throat. The Larkins are so nice. I can't mislead them anymore. I should go. I reach for my eyeglasses and the watch, struggling not to cry.

Just at that moment, Maryellen leans over from the bunk above and hanging upside down says, "Thanks again, Sophie. I'll never forget that it's mostly because of you that we're going on this trip right now. Our Thanksgiving won't be like any other family's in the world. I think it's going to be a great adventure."

Whispers come out of the dark from Beverly and Carolyn, "Me too." . . . "Me too."

Maryellen goes on, "I'm so glad you are here!"

"Me too," says Carolyn.

"Me too," says Beverly.

I swallow the lump in my throat. "Me too," I say. And I mean it.

*✳ Go to page 58.

aryellen has been so friendly and nice to me; I can't bear to go on pretending to her that I'm someone I'm not.

So when she comes back from washing her hands for dinner, I say, "Ellie, listen, I'm really sorry, but I have to go home."

"But why?" Maryellen protests.

"Thank you so much for inviting me to stay," I say. "But in fact, we . . . we might not be moving here after all. I might not see you again."

Maryellen's face falls. "But we're already such good friends!"

"I'll always remember you," I say. "But now I have to go. Please say thank you and good-bye to your family for me."

Maryellen nods. "Good-bye, Sophie," she says. Suddenly, her face brightens, lit up by a great idea. "Let's promise to think of each other whenever we're scared—like when I have to speak in front of a group, and you face something as big as the ocean. It'll make us feel better."

"I promise," I say as I hug Maryellen. "I will if you will."

"You bet!" says Maryellen.

"Good-bye," I say.

"Good-bye," Maryellen says again. We hug and then, reluctantly, I go outside.

I wait until I'm sure that Maryellen is no longer able to see me. Then I step into the trailer and change back into my ski uniform, leaving Carolyn's pretty dress draped neatly over a seat. My finger hesitates over the stopwatch button. Maybe . . .

No! Do it, I say to myself sharply. And I make myself press the button.

∗✳ Turn to page 61.

∗∗✳∗✳✱✳∗✳∗∗

Both my heart and my curiosity tug too hard for me to leave now. So when Mrs. Larkin and the rest of the kids return to the kitchen, I say, "Thank you, ma'am. I can stay."

"Good!" says Mrs. Larkin. "Wash your hands. Dinner is ready."

As I'm washing up, Maryellen's sister Carolyn arrives. She's wearing jeans with the cuffs rolled up and a man's shirt with the shirttails tied at the waist. She smiles at me while Maryellen introduces us. "Nice to meet you, Sophie," she says.

"Nice to meet you, too. Thanks for letting me borrow your dress."

"You're welcome," says Carolyn cheerfully.

All of us children sit at the kitchen table, and Tom asks, "What's for dinner, Mom?"

"Meat loaf," announces Mrs. Larkin.

"My favorite!" we hear someone say.

"That's Dad!" says Beverly. Scooter starts to bark, and everyone is talking at once.

"Dad's home!"

"Dad! Dad! Dad!" crows Mikey.

Mr. Larkin comes in the kitchen door and gives

Mrs. Larkin a big kiss. "Hello, beautiful," he says. "Hi, kids." Then he beams at me. "Well, hello there."

"Dad, meet Sophie," says Maryellen.

"How do you do, Miss Sophie?" says Mr. Larkin. He shakes my hand, as if I'm a grown-up, and everyone giggles. "How did a nice girl like you fall in with a bunch of hooligans like this?"

Now I giggle, too.

"She just moved here," says Beverly. "And Mom said she could sleep over tonight."

"That's good," says Mr. Larkin as he washes his hands at the sink. "The more, the merrier, that's what I say."

Mrs. Larkin takes a delicious-smelling meat loaf out of the oven—they don't seem to have a microwave—and after she has served us, she puts the used serving knife and fork in the sink and fills it with sudsy water. I guess they don't have a dishwasher, either.

"How'd your geography quiz go, sport?" Mr. Larkin asks Maryellen.

"A minus!" says Maryellen.

"That's my girl!" says Mr. Larkin. As we all start eating, Mr. Larkin suddenly puts down his fork and

looks up. "Hey, kids, it's Tuesday night—you know what that means."

I practically jump a foot in the air, because everyone shouts out, "Hi-yo, Silver! Awaa-a-ay!"

Maryellen grins at me. "On Tuesdays, we have dessert in the living room while we watch *The Lone Ranger* on TV."

After dinner, while we clear the table, Mrs. Larkin opens the refrigerator, takes out some cream, and whips it into froth with a hand-powered eggbeater. My mouth starts to water when I see her spoon the whipped cream on top of chocolate pudding. We carry our bowls of pudding into the living room, and we kids sit on the floor in front of the television, while Mr. and Mrs. Larkin settle onto the couch.

The TV screen is small, but the cabinet it's in is huge. Mr. and Mrs. Larkin cheer for the Lone Ranger and Tonto and shout with the rest of us, "Hi-yo, Silver!" Scooter joins in too, howling to show that he's paying attention. The whole scene is sort of wild and chaotic, but it's also really, really fun. When I do go home, I think I'm going to suggest that my whole family watch TV together. It'd be great if we could all laugh at the

✲✻✱✲✱✻✱✲

same show, the way the Larkins do.

After the TV show, Mr. Larkin helps Tom and Mikey construct a cabin out of Lincoln Logs. Carolyn practices piano, and Beverly makes a necklace for herself out of plastic beads that pop together. Maryellen makes a Thanksgiving card for her grandparents. She sketches herself holding a cornucopia of fruit. In the background, a very funny-looking turkey is running away, its feathers flying off.

"That's really good," I tell her.

Maryellen grins. "I love to doodle. If there were a class in doodling at school, I'd get an A plus in it." She sighs, and her grin fades to a frown.

"What's the matter?" I ask.

"Oh, speaking of school reminds me that I have to present a report to my class tomorrow," she says in a voice full of dread. "We're all supposed to speak about something great about Daytona Beach, something that we're thankful for, since Thanksgiving is coming." She shivers. "I know exactly how you feel about being scared of the ocean. I'm scared stiff of standing up in front of everyone."

Beverly pulls two beads apart with a popping

sound. "I bet it'll be just like your polio show," she says, "and you'll freeze up."

Maryellen groans.

"Maybe I could help," I offer. "You could practice your presentation in front of me."

"Let's try it!" says Maryellen. "Come on, let's go to my room."

✳ *Turn to page 71.*

ise and shine!" Mr. Larkin hollers. It's the next morning, and he's rousting us out of bed. "Pancakes for all. Report to the kitchen, troops."

Maryellen, Beverly, Carolyn, and I stumble to the kitchen, rubbing the sleep dust from our eyes. But somehow the scent of hot maple syrup wakes us right up and soon we're devouring sky-high stacks of buttery pancakes. Mr. Larkin, wearing a ruffled apron, is flipping fresh pancakes onto our plates when Maryellen's eldest sister Joan and her husband Jerry arrive.

"Joan and Jerry, meet Sophie," says Mr. Larkin, "who, luckily for us, could use a ride to Washington, D.C."

Joan smiles, and Jerry winks at me. "Hi, Sophie!" they say.

"Pull up a chair," says Mr. Larkin, though the breakfast nook is already cheerfully crowded and noisy and sticky with syrup. "Squeeze in."

"Speaking of squeezing," says Jerry, "won't it be a squeeze fitting all of you into the station wagon?"

"No, there'll be plenty of room. Remember, Scooter's not going," jokes Joan as she bends down to

pat the pudgy dachshund, who wags his tail and licks her hand.

But later, amid all the happy bustle of loading up, I see that we *are* going to be terribly crowded in the station wagon. Even though Carolyn has good-naturedly volunteered to sit in the way-back seat, surrounded by luggage, and Mikey will sit in the front seat between Mr. and Mrs. Larkin, that still leaves Maryellen, Beverly, Tom, and me to squeeze onto the middle seat. Since there are no seat belts, I figure that the four of us will be wedged together all the way from Florida to Washington, D.C.

Of course, *I* have a different way of traveling.

My heart sinks as I realize something sad: Maybe the time has come for me to use the watch and go home. But I realize something wonderful, too: Even though I've spent barely one day with the Larkins, they've changed my whole outlook. If Maryellen can be forgiven for her mistakes and even laugh at them, maybe I can, too. And if the Larkins believe that I'm "independent and enterprising," maybe I really am.

The Larkins have built up my confidence and self-respect and made me feel good about who I am.

∗∗∗∗∗✷✻✷∗∗∗∗∗

Am I ready to go back and stand up for myself?

*** *To go home now,
turn to page 63.*

*** *To go on the trip with Maryellen's family,
turn to page 65.*

woosh . . . When I feel myself on solid ground again and the dizzy feeling stops, I blink and look around. I'm on the ski-race awards platform, with Mom's arm around me. My teammates are talking about me, frowning at me as if I'm a cheat and a liar. I suddenly see what Maryellen meant; it's scary to stand up in front of a bunch of people and speak your mind! But thinking of Maryellen steadies me, so even though I feel as if I'm plunging into the terrifying ocean, I summon my courage and say, "Stop, everybody. Listen to me."

To my surprise, they do.

"I did not cheat," I say, clearly and firmly. "I only made an honest mistake."

∗

Later, after we've been home from the ski mountain for a while, I'm lying on my bed looking at the glow-in-the-dark stars on the ceiling when Emma comes in.

"Hey," she says as she sits on her bed.

"Hey," I say, sitting up.

"Listen," Emma and I begin at the same moment. It usually makes us smile when we do that, but right now, we're too tense.

"You first," I say.

"I just want to say that I'm really sorry, Sophie," Emma says. "I saw you take the shortcut, but I shouldn't have just assumed that you did it on purpose. I never should have accused you of—" She stops.

"Cheating?" I supply the terrible word.

Emma nods, looking miserable. "I should have known you just made an honest mistake."

I nod. "I guess you just made an honest mistake, too."

"Yeah," says Emma. "Big time." She looks at me intently. "So, are we okay?"

"You bet," I say, just the way Maryellen would. I'm happy and relieved.

"Phew," says Emma. "Good. I was sort of afraid you'd never speak to me again."

"No such luck." I think of how I'm going to tell Emma the news that I want to quit the ski team. I grin at her and say, "In fact, watch out. I plan to speak up a *lot* from now on!"

✳ The End ✳

To read this story another way and see how different choices lead to a different ending, turn back to page 46.

All aboard!" calls Mr. Larkin cheerfully.

I wait while Carolyn, Beverly, and Tom clamber into the car. Then quietly but firmly, I say, "Thank you, Mr. Larkin. It was really nice of you to offer me a ride to Washington. But I think Joan and Jerry should call me a taxi, and I should go to the airport and use my ticket home." I don't say that my "ticket home" is a watch!

"No, Sophie!" says Maryellen. "Don't go!"

I hug her without speaking, and Mr. Larkin puts his arm around her shoulders to comfort her. He looks genuinely sorry as he says to me, "Very well, Sophie. If you're sure."

I nod. I'm sorry, too, but I say, "I really miss my family, and I'd like to spend Thanksgiving with them."

"We understand," says Mrs. Larkin. She is holding Mikey on her hip, but with her free hand, she tousles my hair. "If I were your mother, I'd be terribly sad if you were not with me on Thanksgiving Day."

"Oh, I wish you didn't have to go," says Maryellen. "I've loved getting to know you. I'm so glad I met you."

"I'm glad, too," I say. My voice sounds wobbly. "I'll never forget you."

"And I'll never forget you, either," says my new friend. "I'll think of you every mile of our trip."

"Ellie, sweetie," says Mrs. Larkin gently. "Better get in the car now."

Sadly, Maryellen sighs. She hugs me one last time, and then she and Mr. and Mrs. Larkin get into the station wagon. The car doors slam, the station wagon pulls away, and I wave, calling out, "Good-bye! Thank you! Good-bye!"

Maryellen sticks her head out of the window and waves until the car turns a corner and disappears. Even then I think I can hear her—and Carolyn, Tom, Beverly, and Mikey—calling, "Good-bye, Sophie! Good-bye."

With a heavy heart, I change back into my ski-team uniform and leave Carolyn's clothes neatly folded on her bed. Scooter follows me back to the kitchen and sits on my feet as if to keep me from going away. Joan and Jerry call me a taxi and when it comes, I thank them and say good-bye. The minute the taxi lets me out at the airport, I click the watch.

** Turn to page 74.

****✳❄✳****

I can't bear to say good-bye to Maryellen yet. I get into the car with the rest of the family, and happily wave to Joan and Jerry as we set forth on our way. The station wagon is hauling the Airstream trailer, which has bikes hanging off the end of it. We're quite a caravan!

Just as I expected, Maryellen, Beverly, Tom, and I are squashed in the middle seat, and Mikey is between his parents in the front seat. Maryellen has a notepad and a box of colored pencils on her lap, and Beverly and Tom keep taking pencils out of her box. Beverly is using the red as fingernail polish. Tom gives a green pencil to Mikey, who seems to think it is a stalk of celery because he chews on it while Tom beats out a drumbeat with the purple and the yellow.

"I need my red pencil, Beverly," Maryellen says. "Don't chew on my green pencil, Mikey. Hey! They're pencils, not drumsticks, Tom. You're breaking the points!"

I give Mikey my watch to play with, smoothly taking back the green pencil. "Here, you guys," I say to Beverly and Tom, taking the pencils away from them, too. "Let's play Rock-Paper-Scissors."

✴✳✱✶✱✻✖✻✱✶✱✳✴

Maryellen looks at me gratefully, but it's no sweat for me to distract Beverly and Tom. After a few minutes, they're so absorbed in the game that we switch places so that I can sit next to Maryellen.

"Here are your pencils," I say. "What are you doing with them?"

"Last week, I tried out to be a reporter for our school newspaper and I got rejected," Maryellen explains. "The kids who are editors said that my stories were boring. But I still really want to work on the newspaper. So I'm taking notes about what we see on this trip. Maybe if I get an idea for a really exciting story, I can get a second chance."

I look at her pad. "Your drawings are really good."

"Oh," Maryellen says dismissively, "these are just doodles to help me remember ideas. See? I drew a cow to remind myself to write an article about where our school lunch milk comes from. Won't that be interesting?"

"You know, I think kids would get a bigger kick out of your sketch of a cow," I tell her. "It's really funny! I can practically hear it moo."

"Thanks very *mooooch*," jokes Maryellen. "Speaking

of lunch, when are we going to stop, Dad?"

"Yes," groans Carolyn from the way-back seat. "I'm starving!"

"Me too," say Beverly and Tom.

"Me!" adds Mikey.

"We'll stop at the very next diner we see, kids," says Mr. Larkin.

Out the car window, the flat Florida landscape flows by all green and serene; it is so different from the rocky, steep, up-and-down world I'm used to in Cedar Top, North Carolina. The highway is lined with giant billboards advertising cars and restaurants and beaches and weird attractions like snake farms and alligator ranches. Best of all are the series of signs advertising a shaving cream called Burma Shave. Each line is on a separate sign. I read one aloud as we drive by:

> If harmony
> Is what you crave
> Then get a tuba
> Burma Shave

And another one, a few miles later:

No lady likes
To dance or dine
Accompanied by
A porcupine
Burma Shave

Soon Mr. Larkin pulls off and we go to a diner for lunch. Here's a funny thing: Diners haven't changed since the 1950s. I feel right at home when I see the stools at the long, shiny counter, the booths, and the music selector, napkin dispenser, and ketchup and mustard in squeeze bottles at every table. Even the jukebox looks a lot like the ones I've seen in diners at home.

"Ellie," says Mrs. Larkin, "would you and Sophie take Beverly and the boys to the restroom and help them wash their hands?"

"Okay, kids, let's go," sighs Maryellen. She doesn't sound enthusiastic, and I soon see why. Beverly does pirouettes through the diner all the way to the restroom, dancing to the song that's jangling out of the jukebox. And when we get to the restroom, Tom and Mikey stubbornly refuse to wash their hands. "Come on, boys," says Maryellen, exasperated. "Wash!"

"No," says Tom.

I have an idea. I wet my hands, and then fill them with the foamy soap from the dispenser. Humming, I put some of the bubbles on my chin. Then I pretend to shave them off as I say:

Mr. Larkin's
Friend is Dave
I bet that Dave
Likes Burma Shave

Everyone bursts out laughing, and of course Tom and Mikey can't wait to fill their hands with soap and put bubbles on their faces, too. Soon, without even realizing that they're doing so, they're cheerfully washing their hands—and as an extra bonus, their faces—with lots of soap and water.

"Sophie, you're good with little kids," says Maryellen. "*Really* good."

"Well," I say, mopping Mikey with a paper towel, "as long as nobody minds if they get wet. *Really* wet."

Maryellen laughs. "In Mikey's case, it's an improvement!"

I grin. I never knew that I was good with little kids. At home, the only little kid I see is Daria, who comes to our house with her mom, who is my grandmother's secretarial assistant. Gran is—or was—an archaeologist. She's retired now. Daria's mom is helping her organize and catalog all the boxes of weird bones and broken pots and stuff she's collected in her travels. It's a big job, and I don't blame Daria for getting bored waiting. But one reason why Emma and I aren't particularly happy that our grandmother moved in with us last month is that once Daria wandered into our room and wrecked Emma's laptop. Now when we see Daria coming, we close the door.

I don't tell Maryellen about Daria or the laptop or my grandmother. First of all, Maryellen has never heard of a laptop. And second, I feel sort of bad about how Emma and I have been unforgiving to Daria and unfriendly to Gran. As Maryellen and I herd the little kids back to our table in the diner, a new thought enters my mind: Maybe I could be nicer to Gran and Daria. It might even be fun to try to be friends.

✳✳✶ *Turn to page 76.*

✶✳✳✶✳✶✳✶✳✶✳✳✶

As we get up to leave, Mrs. Larkin says, "Ellie, sweetheart, don't forget it's your turn to put the trash out."

Scooter keeps us company as we gather the kitchen garbage, take it outside, and put it in the trash cans. Paper, glass, cans, and food scraps are all mixed together; evidently there's no recycling pickup in 1955. We each carry a trash can to the end of the driveway.

I look up at the stars and gasp. "Holy cow! The sky is so wide and clear here that even without a telescope I see more constellations than I've ever seen at home."

"Can you teach me the constellations?" Maryellen asks.

"Sure," I say, pointing. "Look, there's the Big Dipper, and Orion's belt, and oh, look, there's Pegasus! I've never seen that constellation before!"

"You know a lot about the stars," says Maryellen.

"I love astronomy," I say. "I want to get a telescope someday."

Maryellen nods. "You're smart. You'll figure out a way."

"Well," I say, "I'm not so good at getting what I want. Last summer I wanted to go to astronomy camp,

but my sister campaigned for ski-training camp, and she won out."

"Why didn't you just go to separate camps?" Maryellen asks.

"Emma and I almost always do everything the same," I say. "It's just easier for our family that way."

Maryellen nods sympathetically. "It's like that a lot in my family, too. Sometimes I feel hemmed in."

As I look at the stars, I have a realization. "You know, the stars stay in their constellations, but they move across the sky. Just because you're in a group, it doesn't mean you're stuck in one place." It occurs to me that it's true about Emma and me, as well. We'll always be a pair—a constellation—but we can still move and change.

"I wish I could change my report," Maryellen says as we go inside.

"What did you write about?" I ask.

"Oh, the Daytona car races," says Maryellen, making a tired-looking face. "They're the most famous thing in Daytona Beach. Probably everybody else wrote about them, too. I hate the thought of everyone staring at me as I present my report. But I also dread

presenting it because I know that it'll probably be just like everyone else's report. *Boring.*"

"Wait!" I say. "I have an idea for how we can make your presentation different from everyone else's, and no one will be looking at you as you present it. Come on!"

✳✳ *Turn to page 78.*

✳✳✳✳✳✳✳✳

woosh! Once again, I feel as if I'm flying . . .

When I open my eyes, I find that I'm back on the ski-race awards platform. Coach Stanislav has a steely expression as he talks to the judge. Everyone else is whispering to one another, and my family looks disappointed and sad. For a second, I think about clicking the stopwatch button, leaving this icy sea of disapproval, and returning to the warm, welcoming, wonderful Larkins, who think the best of me. But then it occurs to me that I'll be letting *them* down if I chicken out now. So I step away from Mom's arm, take a deep breath, and say, "Everyone, please listen to me."

No one does.

So I say again, "Please! Listen!"

They ignore me.

"Hey!" Now everyone stops talking and turns to me. "Listen!" I say. "I deserve a chance to defend myself." I speak with such confidence and authority that everyone looks surprised.

"Go ahead," says the judge.

I stand up straight and tall and say, "You all know me, and you know that I would *never* cheat. All I did was choose the wrong branch of the trail. I made an

honest mistake, and I should be forgiven for it." I hand the watch to the judge. "I didn't win, so I don't deserve this watch. But I'm not a cheater, so I don't deserve to be treated like one."

Everyone listens—even Coach Stanislav. When I'm finished, he says, "Sophie, it took guts to speak up for yourself. Well done."

I look him straight in the eye and say, "Thank you, Coach."

"I'm sorry I doubted you, Sophie," says Emma as she hugs me. "Forgive me."

I hug her back, and then I hug Mom and Dad. My heart is light with relief and happiness.

Emma says, "I'm glad you told us what really happened. That was brave."

I catch a glimpse of the watch in the judge's hand, and I smile, thinking, *Well, I didn't tell **everything** that happened, did I, tricky tick-tock?* I wonder if I'll be brave enough to do *that* someday.

* The End *

To read this story another way and see how different choices lead to a different ending, turn back to page 60.

he sun is setting when we arrive at Maryellen's grandparents' house in the Georgia mountains. We all tumble out of the car, and Grandpop swings Maryellen up into an exuberant hug. As soon as her feet touch the ground, Grandmom hugs her, too. They're all delighted to be together.

"This is Sophie," Maryellen says, patting me on the back.

"My Soapy!" announces Mikey, taking me by the hand to show that I'm his special friend.

Everyone laughs kindly at the way Mikey mispronounces my name, and Grandmom hugs me. She's little and bird-like, not at all like my tall, angular grandmother. "Welcome, Soapy Sophie," she says. "I hope Mikey will share you with us."

"Yes, indeed," says Grandpop. "Any friend of Ellie-girl's is a friend of mine."

"That's a warm welcome," says Mr. Larkin, rubbing his hands together, "which is good because it's cold here."

"Sure is!" says Grandpop proudly. "It's been right cold for a while now, which means—" he grins at Maryellen—"that Ellie's pond is frozen. There's even

snow higher up on the mountain."

"Snow!" the Larkins exclaim with excitement.

I realize, of course, that they almost never see snow in Florida. I shiver, even though I'm not cold because Carolyn has given me jeans, a sweater, and a warm jacket to wear. I shiver because I'm recalling the last time I saw snow, which was the moment when Emma betrayed me.

Grandpop winks at Maryellen. "With all the cold weather, your little pond is frozen hard enough—"

"—to skate on!" Maryellen shouts, her eyes sparkling.

"As long as you're careful and stay near the shore, where it's good and thick," Grandmom adds.

"Come on, Soapy Sophie," says Maryellen, tugging on my arm. "I want to show you *everything*."

✳✱✳ *Turn to page 85.*

aryellen and I work long and hard on her presentation. There's no Internet in 1955, so we use a big set of books called the *World Book Encyclopedia* to look up the facts that we need. Maryellen's skill at sketching comes in very handy, since part of the presentation is going to be visual. She practices presenting her report to me over and over again until it's perfect. By the time we tumble into bed, Beverly and Carolyn are already asleep in their bunks.

The next morning at breakfast, Maryellen and I are both so excited about getting to school that we can hardly eat. Well, actually, I do manage to eat six pieces of bacon. It's so delicious!

Carolyn says, "Sophie, you can take my bike to school today if you like. I won't need it. There's a sock hop in the gym after school today, so I'm getting a ride."

I say, "Thanks!" But when Maryellen and I leave for school, she walks right past the bikes in the carport.

"Aren't we going to ride bikes to school?" I ask.

Maryellen hesitates. "Uh, well, okay," she says. She does not sound enthusiastic.

She slings her book bag with the materials for

her presentation in it over her shoulder, and wheels Carolyn's bike over to me. She sighs and hesitates for a moment, but before I can ask her what's wrong she climbs onto a sleek black bike, and off we go.

It gives me a great feeling of independence to ride a bike to school. What a nice way to start the day: riding along in a sweet-smelling breeze with the morning sunshine on your face. I'm a little nervous about riding without a helmet, but the bike ride is a million times nicer than being crammed onto the noisy, smelly bus I ride at home.

When Maryellen and I pedal into the schoolyard, I notice that the kids are running around and playing outdoor games, using jump ropes, playing hopscotch, or just zooming around playing tag.

"Get a load of you, Larkin," a loud boy in a beanie cap with a propeller on top says to Maryellen as we're parking our bikes in the bike stand. "Don't you know that's a *boy's* bike? Look at the bar. What're you doing riding *that*?"

Maryellen blushes. "Cut it out, Wayne," she says. So this is the "terrible boy" that Beverly mentioned. I can tell that his teasing embarrasses Maryellen; now

I know why she was reluctant to ride bikes this morning. Maryellen states firmly, "I'll get a new *girl's* bike as soon as I save enough money."

"Meanwhile, ditch that one," Wayne goes on. "Girls can't ride boys' bikes."

"They do where I come from," I say loudly. It's not like me to speak up, but I can't stand anybody picking on Maryellen!

"Don't pay any attention to Wayne the Pain," says a girl in a poodle skirt.

"That's right," says a cheerful-looking girl with freckles.

A third girl, with long, dark braids, turns to Wayne and says, "Go away."

Wayne slinks off, and Maryellen introduces me to her three friends. "This is Sophie. She's new. She's from Cedar Top, North Carolina."

I feel a little shy as I say, "Hi, nice to meet you," to Maryellen's friends. But they're really friendly.

"Hi, Sophie. I'm Karen Stohlman," says the girl in the poodle skirt.

"I'm Karen King," says the girl with freckles.

"I'm Angela," says the third girl, the one with the

long, dark braids. "I was new at the beginning of last year, so I know it's confusing at first."

"But don't worry," says Karen King. "If you have any questions, just ask us."

"I bet Ellie asked you a *million* questions when you first got here," says Karen Stohlman. I grin and nod. Karen is right; Maryellen *did* ask me a lot of friendly questions. "Ellie's always curious. Right, Ellie?"

"You bet," says Maryellen. "Like right now, I'm curious about outer space, because that's where I'd like to send Wayne. I'm *so tired* of him teasing me about this bike." She explains to me, "My friend Davy gave it to me when he outgrew it. I'd love a new bike, but bikes are expensive, so I have to ride Davy's old bike until I earn enough money to buy a girl's bike for myself. When I do, I'm going to wrap this one around Wayne."

"Then he can spin that propeller on his beanie and take off," I joke.

We laugh together, and I feel right at home. Any shyness I felt at first has melted away. I realize that I don't have much experience in making friends. I've never had to, because Emma and I have always been such an exclusive duo, such a two-girl team. Maybe

I could try to make new friends when I return to my own time.

We all go inside the school. Maryellen introduces me to her homeroom teacher, Mr. Garcia. He says, "Because it's only a half day of school today, you can be a classroom visitor, and we'll sort out your registration after Thanksgiving break."

The whole class stands, and we recite the Pledge of Allegiance. Then Mr. Garcia sits down at a piano in the classroom, and we all sing "The Star-Spangled Banner."

"All right," says Mr. Garcia after the song. "Who wants to give the first presentation?"

Maryellen looks at me nervously, but I smile and nod to her with encouragement, so she raises her hand and says, "Can—I mean, *may* I go first?"

"Certainly," says Mr. Garcia.

Everyone whispers and giggles in surprise as I turn off the classroom lights and pull down all the window shades to make the room dark. Maryellen stands in the middle of the room, holding a lit flashlight under a piece of construction paper in which she has cut small, star-shaped holes. There on the ceiling of the classroom is the Little Dipper!

"Ahhh," the class sighs with delight.

Maryellen begins. "One of the things I'm most grateful for here in Daytona Beach is our big, beautiful night sky," she says. "Over the ocean, on a clear night, you can see a sky full of stars. This constellation is the Little Dipper. The big star at the end of the handle is the North Star. The North Star marks the way true north, so in the olden days, travelers used it to find their direction." Maryellen puts a different piece of paper over the flashlight. "This constellation is the Big Dipper," she says. She speaks about the Big Dipper for a while, and then she puts a third paper over the flashlight and talks about Pegasus, the flying horse. When she has finished her presentation, Mr. Garcia turns on the lights, and everyone claps.

"Excellent job, Maryellen," says Mr. Garcia. "People have been fascinated by the night sky for centuries. Maybe someday we'll be able to travel into outer space—maybe even to the moon."

Wayne pipes up. "That's impossible!"

I smile. At home, I'm very quiet in the classroom, but now I can't resist saying, "Wayne, I think you're wrong. In fact, I bet scientists will put men on the

moon in less than fifteen years." I remind myself
to tell Maryellen that she might want to be at Cape
Canaveral—which is, after all, only a little way from
Daytona Beach—on July 16, 1969, to see the historic
launch of *Apollo 11*.

"Hmph!" scoffs Wayne. "Well, I'll tell you one thing
for sure—*men* might walk on the moon, but no *girl* will
ever go up in space."

"Oh, I bet you're wrong about that, too," I say,
thinking of the astronaut Sally Ride, who went into
space in 1983.

Maryellen beams at me. She whispers, "That's telling 'em."

As we take our seats, I whisper back to Maryellen,
"I think you've beaten your fear of speaking in front of
people."

"Yes, and it was easy," says Maryellen. "Of course,
it helped that everyone was looking up at the stars, not
at me!"

*⁎✻ **Turn to page 90.**

⁎⁎✻⁎✻⁎✻✻⁎✻⁎⁎✻⁎

aryellen leads me inside the cabin, and as I look around I feel as though I've been carried back into the past again, even further. Grandmom and Grandpop's cabin is even more old-fashioned than the Larkins' house. There's a rocking chair facing a big stone fireplace and a couch with a knitted blanket draped over it. There's a braided rug on the floor, which is made of wide planks of wood. Next to the fireplace, I see a frame full of pencil sketches.

"Aren't those fine?" says Grandpop, when he sees me studying them. "Made for me by Miss Maryellen Larkin, every single one of 'em. Ellie's my correspondent, and the drawings she does on her cards and letters are so good, I framed them so's everybody can see them and admire them as much as I do."

"Oh, Grandpop," says Maryellen. She blushes. I can tell that she is pleased. *It must be nice to have your grandparents be proud of you,* I think. *I wonder if my grandmother will ever be proud of me?*

On the wall next to Maryellen's sketches is a calendar. I stare at the date. What *is* it about November 1955 that rings a bell with me? I rack my brains, but I can*not* remember.

We eat dinner in front of the fireplace and it's great
fun, because we have an indoor wienie roast, cooking
our hot dogs on sticks over the fire. Grandmom lets
me roast hot dogs for Mikey and Tom and load the hot
dogs up sloppily with gobs of ketchup and homemade
relish, which of course drips onto their shirts as they
eat. Maryellen rolls her eyes, but nobody fusses when
Mikey spills popcorn all over the floor. Grandmom
sweeps it into the fireplace and we all go right on having fun.

As a special treat, Maryellen and I are going to
sleep in the trailer. "Just the two of us!" says Maryellen
happily. So after dinner we wash our hands and faces,
brush our teeth, and, as Grandpop says, "scamper to
the camper."

After the warmth and brightness of the cabin, the
camper is a bit chilly and dark. But when Maryellen
turns on the light, I can see that the trailer is a wonder-
fully compact house-on-wheels. It has everything: a
kitchen with a tiny sink, stove, refrigerator, and cabi-
nets, a hallway to a bedroom, and a bathroom that even
has a bathtub and shower. Maryellen and I hurry into
our pajamas and then snuggle into our sleeping bags.

When Maryellen turns off the light, I look out the big window and gasp. "Whoa."

"What?" asks Maryellen.

"I've never seen so *many* stars before!" I say. "Where I come from, there are so many streetlights that the stars are hidden. Look! There's the Big Dipper, and the Little Dipper, and Orion's belt."

"You sure know the constellations," says Maryellen. "You're an expert."

"Well, thanks!" I say. I've never thought of myself as an expert at anything. I mean, I've always been one half of a pair—Emma-n-Sophie, a package deal. And usually, I just do what Emma wants to do. "I wish I had a telescope, so I could really study the stars and get good at identifying them."

"I don't know *what* I'm good at," says Maryellen. "It's hard to be outstanding when you're always standing in the middle of a crowd like my family." She smiles. "Is there such a thing as an *opposite* telescope? Because I'd like to make things that are near look far away—like Beverly, Tom, and Mikey, for instance. Sometimes I feel like we're an eight-legged monster, stuck together forever and ever."

I know exactly what Maryellen means; I often feel as if Emma and I are glued together.

Maryellen sounds a little sheepish as she admits, "I suppose it's silly, but sometimes I like to pretend I'm someone famous like Debbie Reynolds, or a figure skater in the Ice Capades. The problem is, it's hard to imagine myself as anyone glamorous when Beverly, Tom, and Mikey are around demanding my attention and pestering the life out of me." She sighs.

"I have an idea," I tell her. "Tomorrow morning, before anyone else is awake, let's have an adventure, just the two of us. Maybe we could go for a walk in the woods."

"You bet!" says Maryellen.

"Good night, then," I say.

"Good night!"

Silently, I wave good night to the stars, too.

✱

Before I know it, Maryellen is shaking me awake. "Get dressed," she says. "Come on! It's time for our adventure."

"Where are we going?" I ask groggily.

"You'll see," says Maryellen with a mischievous, mysterious twinkle.

We pull on our clothes. Then, quietly, quietly, Maryellen opens the door of the camper, and we sneak away, into the woods.

✱ *Turn to page 93.*

Later, Maryellen and I are walking home from school. For a while, the two Karens and Angela walk with us.

"Ellie," says Karen King, "your presentation was by far the best. I practically fell asleep during Wayne's presentation about the car races. Whenever he went *vroom*, I went *snore*."

"I liked your report about the educator Mary McLeod Bethune," I tell Angela. "I wrote a report about her last February for Black History Month. It's cool that she lived in Daytona Beach and that the college for girls that she started is still here."

"She died this past May," says Angela, "so I didn't get to meet her, but I interviewed some people who knew her."

"I liked your report about Jackie Robinson," says Maryellen to Karen Stohlman. "I knew that he and the Dodgers won the World Series this year, but I didn't know he used to come here to Daytona Beach for spring training."

Maryellen turns and grins at me. "Maybe Daytona Beach isn't so dull after all! I mean, of course I'm still curious about places I've never been, but now I know

that my hometown is worth exploring. It has interesting people in it, too."

I wonder if I've overlooked interesting people in *my* hometown, too—maybe even in my *home*. I've just sort of assumed that my grandmother isn't very interesting because she's gray-haired and quiet and the dusty stuff she brought with her looks ancient and weird. But my mom says Gran used to be an archaeology professor, and she's highly respected in her field, and the ancient, weird things are actually rare artifacts that Gran herself found on digs all over the country. Now Gran and Daria's mother are organizing the things to donate them to a museum.

Gran might have some fascinating stories to tell. Maybe I jumped to a conclusion about her, just the way people jumped to a conclusion about me, thinking I cheated in the ski race. Maryellen said she hates it when people just assume she's fragile because she had polio. Maybe *I've* been making wrong assumptions, too.

The two Karens and Angela split off in different directions to head to their homes, so we say good-bye. Maryellen and I continue on toward the Larkins' house,

but with every step, I find myself asking, should I go home now and get to know my grandmother?

> *** To go home,*
> *turn to page 95.*

> *** To stay,*
> *turn to page 102.*

aryellen leads me up a narrow trail that twists its way between pine trees. The higher we go, the more snow there is on the pine trees, and the thicker the cushion of snow on the ground. We go up and up, cross a snowy road as narrow and rutted as a path, and then step into a little clearing.

"Ah!" I breathe.

"Welcome to my pond," says Maryellen. "Isn't it perfect?"

I nod. The small, secret pond seems almost magical, as if it were enchanted and frozen in time. Pine trees circle it and stoop toward it protectively, because they are weighted down with snow. There's a tumbledown shed next to the pond, and inside it we find a jumble of ice skates, old wooden skis, boots, ski poles, shovels, pails, and a canvas sack for carrying firewood.

I shudder when I see the skis. And when Maryellen says, "Do you ski?" I answer brusquely, "No." *I don't want to, anyway*, I think to myself.

"That's okay. Neither do I," says Maryellen. "But I thought maybe you and I could try it out today. You know, just slip and slide around on the skis a little bit, just for fun. We could imagine that we're Olympic

skiers! What do you think?"

I hesitate.

"If you don't want to ski, we could skate," says
Maryellen, picking up a pair of skates. She turns to me.
"Which do you want to do?"

✻✻ *To skate with Maryellen,
turn to page 97.*

✻✻ *To ski with Maryellen,
turn to page 107.*

I decide yes. It is time to go home and make friends with Gran.

When we get to the Larkins' house, I take a deep breath. "Ellie," I say. "I'm going to leave now."

"Okay," says Maryellen cheerily. "But come back later. It'd be fun if you could spend the night again."

Maryellen has misunderstood me, and it makes my heart hurt to explain what I mean by "leave."

"Thanks, but I don't think I can come back," I tell her. "Tomorrow is Thanksgiving, and I'll be traveling home to Cedar Top." I don't say that my vehicle is my watch, and that my trip will be going forward sixty years in time. Instead, I force myself to say, "In fact, my family might stay in Cedar Top and not move here after all. So I had better say good-bye."

"Good-bye?" asks Maryellen. "For good?"

I nod. I'm too sad to speak.

Maryellen sounds sad too as she says, "I'll never forget you, Sophie."

"I won't forget you, either," I say. "We may not see each other, but we'll be friends forever, right?"

"You bet," says Maryellen.

We hug. Then slowly, reluctantly, Maryellen goes

inside her house. When she is gone, I duck into the trailer.

My hands are sort of shaky as I put my ski uniform back on and hang Carolyn's dress on a hanger. I'm worried about going home, but I'm partly excited, too. I decide that after I clear up the misunderstanding about the ski race, the first thing I'll do is ask Gran to tell me all about her artifacts—where she found them, what they were used for, and why they're important. I bet Emma and Mom and Dad will be interested, too. It would be fun for all of us to listen to Gran's stories and to be together some evening, like the Larkins were when they watched *The Lone Ranger* on TV. I smile, thinking, *I'll do what Ellie did when she first met me: I'll ask Gran a million questions!*

I click the watch.

✳ The End ✳

To read this story another way and see how different choices lead to a different ending, turn back to page 92.

would much rather skate," I tell her, turning my back on the skis.

"Okay," says Maryellen.

We find skates that fit pretty well, and soon we are skating and clearing the snow off the ice with a shovel and broom as we go. When we've cleared a small area, we skate holding hands, around and around, bending forward when we come to an overhanging pine bough, standing straight when we're in the clear. We're careful to stay away from the middle of the pond in case the ice is thin there. There's no sound but the *scritch, scritch* of our skates and the *whoosh* of the pines in the wind.

"See what I mean?" Maryellen asks quietly. "It's easy to imagine that we're skaters in the Ice Capades or in an old-fashioned movie, isn't it!"

I nod. She's right, it's wonderful, until—

"There you are!" Beverly's indignant voice pierces the silence, jolting Maryellen and me back into reality. "You're mean, Ellie Larkin, to sneak off without telling us." Three stout little figures appear on the bank of the pond: Beverly, Tom, and Mikey, all so bundled up that they are as big around as they are tall.

"You three shouldn't have come all this way by

yourselves," scolds Maryellen. "How'd you find us, anyway?"

"We followed your boot prints," says Beverly. "*We* want to skate, too."

"No," says Maryellen. "This is just for Sophie and me."

"You can't hog skating," says Beverly. "And you're not supposed to hog Sophie, either. She's a friend of all of us. Grandmom said so."

"Oh, all right," says Maryellen. "Go ahead and skate. Sophie and I are finished." She flings her arm out over the pond. "It's all yours."

"But we want to skate with *you*," insists Beverly.

"No," says Maryellen again. "There aren't enough skates anyway. You'll have to wear these, and the boys will have to slide around in their boots. Come on, Sophie."

The two little boys wibble-wobble out onto the ice, clutching at each other to stay on their feet. Maryellen and I skate past them to the edge, and she plunks down on the ground. She unlaces her skates, pulls them off, and hands them to Beverly. I take my skates off more slowly. Beverly has one of Maryellen's skates on and

I'm returning my skates to the shed when suddenly we hear a terrifying howl.

I rush out of the shed and go rigid with horror. Tom is howling because *Mikey has fallen through the ice.*

"Help, help, help!" Tom wails, starting to cry.

My heart beats fast with fear as Maryellen and I slip and slide in our boots on the ice. "Don't get too near the middle!" I caution. "If Mikey fell through, you will, too."

When we reach the boys, I pull Tom away from the gaping hole and gently prod him to the safer, thicker ice, where Beverly leads him safely to the bank. I turn back to see Maryellen lying on her stomach, reaching her arms out to Mikey. I lie behind her and hold on to her feet so that she won't fall into the hole, too.

"Come on, Mikey," Maryellen coaxes. "Reach out to me. That's it—that's the way. That's a brave boy." Maryellen grabs Mikey's hands, then hooks her hands under his arms and slowly hauls him out of the water.

We're breathless for a moment, and then we carry Mikey between us to the bank of the pond. He's soaked through to the skin, and he is so cold that he's shivering and shaking.

"What'll we do?" moans Beverly, clutching Tom.

"We're going to get Mikey back to the cabin as quickly as possible," says Maryellen. She turns to me and says, "Get the canvas sack out of the shed. We'll take turns carrying him in that. He's heavy, especially now that he's wet, but if we use the sack as a sling, I think we can manage."

I run to the shed to get the sack. In the shed, I see the skis and boots—and I know what I must do. Maryellen bravely saved Mikey from the ice; now *I* must save him from hypothermia. Quickly, I put on the boots and skis, grab some poles, and tie the sack around me like a sling. "Ellie," I call, skiing toward her, "Put Mikey in the sling, and I'll ski him back to the cabin. That'll be faster than walking."

Maryellen looks surprised. "But you said you don't ski," she says.

"Never mind that now," I say. "I can ski. Please trust me."

Maryellen doesn't argue. She puts Mikey in the sling, and at first I'm afraid I will tip over from his weight. For a little guy, he is heavy. But I get my balance and shove off.

The boots are too big, and they're stiff and

awkward. The skis—which are really meant for down-hill, not cross-country skiing—are clunky and hard to maneuver. But I'm determined. Maryellen, Beverly, and Tom trot behind me, but they can't keep up, and soon I'm alone, following the trail we made with our boot prints in the snow, skiing as fast as I can. All I can think is, *I've got to get Mikey to warmth.*

I'm so out of breath that I can't think anymore. All I can do is focus all my strength on skiing and not falling. The trail twists and turns, but it leads steadily downhill and at last I see smoke coming out of the chimney of the cabin. "We made it, Mikey," I whisper.

"Soapy," says Mikey. "My."

"That's right, Mikey," I say. "Oh, *my.*"

✳✳✻ Turn to page 110.

Before I come to a decision about staying or going, Maryellen and I walk past a new store opening up. There are trees in pots on the sidewalk outside the store, and inside we can see a colorful riot of flowers and plants. The flowers are so bright and gorgeous, I imagine that I can even smell their perfume through the glass window! Then something else in the window catches my eye.

"Look at that," I say, tugging on Maryellen's sleeve and then pointing to a sign in the window of the store:

- Enter our contest.
- Think up a name and a slogan
  for our new store.
- Draw a logo.
- You could win a cash prize!

"You should enter that contest, Ellie," I say. "You're great at sketching! If you win, you could buy a new bike."

"I do love to sketch," says Maryellen. "And it would be fun to think up a name and a slogan, especially for a place that sells trees and plants."

"Have you ever entered a contest before?" I ask.

"Oh, sure," says Maryellen. "You know how popular contests are. Hey, maybe you should enter, too, and try to win money for your telescope."

"Nope, not me," I say. "Thanks, but I'm no good at drawing. This contest has your name written all over it."

"You bet!" says Maryellen enthusiastically.

We're both so excited that we walk faster, chatting about ideas all the way. When we return to the Larkins' house, we practically fly to Maryellen's room. The box of construction paper and markers we used for her star presentation is still there, sort of shoved under Beverly's bunk, so we plunk ourselves down on the floor. There's not much space between the beds, so we're squashed knee-to-knee. Maryellen draws a few doodles while we swap ideas.

Beverly appears, followed by Scooter. Beverly's cardboard crown is askew, but she is still queenly as she asks, "What're you doing?"

"Nothing," says Maryellen.

Beverly looks stubborn. I can tell she's not going to go away, so I say, "We're working on an art project."

"Yes," says Maryellen. "And it's important. So go, and please take Scooter with you. It's too crowded in here."

"You can't make me go," says Beverly crossly. "This is my room, too."

Maryellen sighs, exasperated. "Okay, stay, Queen Beverly. But don't bother us."

Beverly's getting red in the face. "Here, Beverly," I say, handing her a sheet of construction paper and a few markers. "Would you draw a ballerina for me?"

"Yes," says Beverly. "I'll draw *me*." She sits cross-legged on her bed and is soon happily absorbed in her drawing.

"Thanks, Sophie," says Maryellen with a grateful grin. "You're good with little kids." She asks me, "Do you have to share a room with your sister?"

"I do now," I say. "When my grandmother moved in with us, I moved into my sister Emma's room. We haven't been getting along very well ever since."

"Too crowded?" asks Maryellen sympathetically.

I nod. "All our stuff is crammed together," I say. "And Emma doesn't like the star stuff I put up." Whenever I come into the room, Emma puts her

earphones on and retreats into her music as if I'm not there. I don't tell Maryellen that, because I haven't seen even one kid with earphones in Maryellen's time.

"Beverly and I used to share this room with Tom and Mikey," says Maryellen. "I really wanted Carolyn and Joan to move in so that this could be an all-girls room. But before the older girls would agree to move, I had to learn to be more tidy."

"Sharing a room is hard," I say. "It's been a big change for Emma and me."

"Well," says Maryellen, "I sure had to change. I had to turn over a new leaf." Suddenly, Maryellen looks at me, her face lit with joy. "That's it!" she says. "That's the perfect name for the new plant store." Quick as a wink, she sketches a tree branch—it's amazing how she can draw one with just a few strokes—and then she draws big leaves on it. On one leaf she prints **A NEW LEAF.**

"A name and logo—that's brilliant!" I exclaim.

"Thanks! Now we need a slogan," says Maryellen.

"The branch you drew is really good," I say. "I like the way the big limb branches out into lots of littler ones."

Maryellen grabs me in a big hug. "Sophie, you're

✳✱✳✱✳✳✱✳✱✳

a genius!" she exclaims. "You just gave me a great idea for a slogan."

Quickly, she adds to her sign, and then holds it up.

Now, above the tree limb, in letters decorated with leaves, it says, "**Branch out! Shop at**" and the words **A NEW LEAF** appear on the big leaf under the limb.

"*You're* the genius," I say.

Beverly leans down and looks over Maryellen's shoulder at her sketch. "That's good," she says, bestowing royal approval.

But Maryellen isn't satisfied. She works hard, drawing and redrawing, printing and reprinting, until her sign is just the way she wants it. She's adding finishing touches to her work when the phone rings.

✲✲ Turn to page 111.

It is clear to me that Maryellen would really like to ski. So, even though the last time I was on skis was the worst day of my life and part of me never wants to put skis on ever again, I say, "Okay. Let's ski."

"Great!" says Maryellen.

We pull dusty old boots and skis and poles out of the tangle of equipment on the floor of the little shed, and pretty soon, both Maryellen and I are strapped into our skis. They weigh a ton! And the boots do, too. This equipment is not meant for cross-country skiing, and it's not at all like the ski equipment I'm used to at home. I feel like I've got cement blocks on my feet.

Maryellen grins. "Here goes nothing," she says, clomping clumsily over to the pond. "Let's begin by skiing on the pond," she says. "It's flat, so we can get used to our skis."

"Okay," I say. I'm not much better on my skis than Maryellen is at first. We both wobble and weave our way to the pond, inch our way onto the ice, and *plonk!* We fall down hard. For some reason, this makes us both laugh uproariously. The more I laugh, the more the tight knot that I've had in my chest whenever I've even *thought* about skiing loosens. Maryellen has

reminded me that skiing is, after all, supposed to be fun—something I had forgotten in all the misery of the ski race and the pressure of being on the ski team.

"Come on," I say to Maryellen, pulling her to her feet. "Try this," I say. Slowly, I push forward on my skis as I was taught to do. Maryellen copies me, and soon she is skiing smoothly, too.

"Ready for a hill?" I ask.

"You bet!" Maryellen nods.

We herringbone our way up the bank of the pond to the trail, and I show Maryellen how to squat down in a snowplow, the tips of her skis pointing in. We push off, and down the trail we go. I'm steady as a rock, and Maryellen is doing pretty well, too, for a first-timer. We round a curve, pick up speed, and swoop across the snow. I see a bump and fly over it, landing with a soft thump. *Ahh*, it feels wonderful!

It occurs to me that maybe, when I go back home, I could tell Emma that I miss skiing just for fun. Maybe we could start going to the ski mountain early and ski one or two runs before practice begins every day, just the two of us, just skiing the way we used to—the way I love to. I bet Emma will say yes.

"Hey," pants Maryellen as she catches up to me. "Are you sure you haven't skied before?"

"I have," I admit. "But I thought I didn't like it. Now, thanks to you, I remember how much I love it." I smile. "Come on, Ellie—let's ski some more."

✳ **Turn to page 115.**

Later, we are all sitting around the fire after Thanksgiving dinner, feeling warm and cozy and full. Mikey is leaning against me, dozing.

Maryellen says, "I'll tell you what I'm most grateful for this Thanksgiving: Sophie. She helped me save Mikey's life today."

Grandmom slips her arm around my shoulder.

"Hear, hear," says Mr. Larkin. "I think we all agree that Ellie is an outstanding sister and Sophie is an outstanding friend. In fact, I move that we elect Sophie as an honorary Larkin. All in favor, say, 'Aye.'"

"Aye!" says everyone.

"My," sighs Mikey, practically asleep. "My Soapy."

"That makes it unanimous," says Mr. Larkin.

I'm awfully proud to be an honorary member of the Larkin family. What a great feeling it is to be included.

I wonder: If Emma and I tried to include my grandmother, would she feel more like a member of our family? When I go home, I should try to find out.

✷✷ Turn to page 115.

✳✷✳✷✳✷✷✳✷✳✷

A minute later, Mrs. Larkin pops her head into the room. "Ellie," she says, "that was Carolyn on the phone. She forgot her ticket to the sock hop. I've got my hands full with Tom and Mikey, and with making pies for Thanksgiving. May I ask you to find Carolyn's ticket and then take it to her? She'll meet you at the high school gym, where the sock hop is being held."

"Sure, Mom," says Maryellen. "Sophie and I have to take this sign that I made to the new plant store, anyway."

"I'm coming, too," says Queen Beverly.

"All right, dear," says Mrs. Larkin, already out the door. "Thanks, girls."

Maryellen and I search hard, but it is Beverly who finally finds Carolyn's ticket in her top drawer hidden under bobby pins, cold cream, fingernail polish, Audrey-Hepburn-ish sunglasses, and headscarves. "I'll give the ticket to Carolyn," says Beverly proudly as the three of us set out.

When we drop off Maryellen's sign at the new plant store, the owner is surprised at how young Maryellen is, but he asks Maryellen to write her name and phone number on the back.

****❄****

"Maybe you'll win the contest, Ellie!" says Beverly.

Maryellen shrugs and smiles. "I doubt it. Probably a grown-up artist will win. But it was fun to make the sign, anyway."

When we get to the high school, we find Carolyn waiting in the hall just outside the gym.

"You guys are lifesavers!" says Carolyn when Beverly gives her the ticket.

"Beverly found it all by herself," I say, and Beverly rewards me with a big smile.

"Thank you, Queen Beverly," says Carolyn. She winks at Maryellen and me, and goes into the dance. Maryellen, Beverly, and I peer through the open doors at the sock hop. Old-time rock 'n' roll music shakes the gym and makes the floor thump under my feet. I can see why the dance is called a sock hop: Shoes are lined up along the walls, and the kids on the dance floor are dancing in their socks. I mean, they are *really* dancing, like on TV dancing-contest shows. Carolyn is dancing with a boy who expertly twirls her under his arm. One time, I saw my cousin Tucker's high school dance, and it was nothing like this. At that dance, the kids were all in jeans, the gym was dark with pulsating colored

lights, and most of the kids were slouching in groups
next to the walls, shouting at one another to be heard
over the deafening music. The kids who were on the
dance floor were mostly just jumping up and down,
not exactly dancing. But at Carolyn's dance, the girls
are wearing pretty, swirly dresses like the one Carolyn
loaned to me, and the boys are wearing letter sweaters
or jackets and ties. The gym is decorated with loops
of colorful crepe paper strung between the basketball
hoops and the windows.

"Do you think it looks like fun?" Maryellen asks
me.

I nod. "Do you?"

"Mmm, well, yes, I guess so," says Maryellen.
"Except for having to dance with a boy. I mean, what if
you had to dance with a boy like Wayne?" She makes a
horrified face, and Beverly and I laugh.

"Some girls at my school are already interested in
boys," I say. "They think that I should be, too."

Maryellen looks skeptical. "I think it's going to be a
long, *long* time before I'm interested in boys."

Beverly pipes up, "But don't you want to get married, like Joan?"

"Joan's *nineteen*," says Maryellen, as if that's old.

I'm surprised. In the twenty-first century—where *I* live, anyway—most girls would think nineteen is very young to be married.

"Nineteen is a long way off," Maryellen continues. "First I want to go to college. Then, I really want to be an artist when I grow up."

"You're *already* an artist," I say, as we share a smile.

** Turn to page 117.

Later that night, when Maryellen and I are in our sleeping bags in the camper, she asks, "Why did you tell me at first that you didn't ski?"

I take a deep breath. "Just before I came here, I was accused of cheating in a ski race. I never wanted to ski again."

"Why would anyone ever think that you cheated?" asks Maryellen.

"I made a mistake and skied down the wrong trail. It turned out to be a shortcut, so I won the race," I explain. "My sister thought that I cheated. And my coach doesn't trust me, because I played a trick on him once."

"But didn't you tell everyone that it was just a mistake?" Maryellen asks.

"I tried, but I bungled it. I was too confused and humiliated. It seemed as though everyone jumped to a conclusion and I couldn't stop them. I was too chicken to fight for myself."

"You are not a *bit* chicken," says Maryellen firmly.

"Oh, yes, I am. I can't even tell my sister that I don't want to be on the ski team. I don't like the uniforms, I don't like the competition, and I don't like how serious

skiing has become for us—but she does." I pause. "But I'm afraid that if I tell her that I want to quit the ski team, she'll be hurt and disappointed."

Maryellen thinks for a moment. Then she says, "Your sister may be disappointed, but she deserves to know the truth, and you deserve to tell it. I *know* that you're brave enough to speak up for yourself."

I straighten my shoulders a bit. When Maryellen calls me brave, I *feel* brave.

"You deserve a second chance to explain what happened in the ski race," she continues. "When you go home, you need to set the record straight, especially with your sister. Promise me that you will."

"I promise," I say, hoping that I'll have the nerve.

*⁎✳ To stay with Maryellen,
turn to page 121.

*⁎✳ To go home and tell Emma the truth,
turn to page 126.

⁎✳*✳✳*✳*⁎*

e're hot and sweaty when we get back to the Larkins' house, so I guess I should be glad when Mrs. Larkin says, "Okay, troops! Time for the beach." She uses the back of her wrist to push her hair off her forehead, because her hands are floury. "I could use a swim after being elbow-deep in apple pie and pumpkin pie for tomorrow's dinner. Go put your suits on."

Maryellen waits until we're in her bedroom before she says kindly, "Sophie, you don't have to swim, you know, if you don't feel ready."

I grin, but it's wobbly. I tell myself firmly that Maryellen faced her fear at school this morning, so maybe today's the day for me to face mine, too.

Maryellen finds a bathing suit of Carolyn's that will fit me, and gives me a rubber bathing cap decorated with fish. I try it on and look at myself in the mirror. The cap's really funny-looking. It has a strap that goes under my chin and fastens to a snap near my ear. I look bald in it!

Maryellen, Beverly, and I help Mrs. Larkin load the station wagon and then we climb into the car with Tom, Mikey, and Scooter, who manages to be in the way no matter where he sits. It's a short drive to the beach,

only two blocks. When we get there, I help unload the car and carry all the stuff across the hot sand. Then I help Mrs. Larkin set up a chair for herself under the big beach umbrella, and I spread a towel by her feet. I set Mikey up with a pail and shovel. But even with all those delaying tactics, I can't postpone facing the ocean any longer.

I take off my eyeglasses and take sweet little Tom by the hand. Little does he know that *he* is the one steadying and supporting *me* as we walk toward the waves.

Boom! Crash! Yikes, the waves are even bigger and more thunderous than I remembered.

"Don't be scared, Sophie," says Tom. He looks so worried for me that I have to smile at him.

"Okay now, Sophie," says Maryellen. "You don't have to plunge in, but are you ready to get your feet wet?"

I nod, swallowing hard.

Maryellen takes me by one hand and Tom's still holding the other. Beverly follows as I walk forward until the waves lick my feet and curl up around my ankles. The water is not very cold, so I step forward

again, until the water is up to my knees.

"Hurray for Sophie!" cheers Maryellen, and Tom and Beverly cheer, too. Then Maryellen says, "Good job, Sophie."

I wish I could say that after a few minutes I'm running and diving headfirst into the waves just as fearlessly as Maryellen. But that wouldn't be true. Instead, I spend some time splashing in the shallows with Tom, where I feel comfortable, and then Mrs. Larkin holds me as I float on my back in waist-deep water. Once, a wave lifts me up and I feel weightless. Is this how it feels for astronauts? I try it again—and get salt water up my nose. Clearly, it's going to take me a while to feel at ease in the ocean. I'm really happier using my bathing cap as a pail for water to fill the moat around the sand castle that Tom, Mikey, and Queen Beverly are building.

"It's nice of you to help them," says Maryellen, joining us.

"The bathing cap looks better full of water than it does on my head," I joke.

"Maybe you can be a babysitter to earn money for your telescope," says Maryellen.

"Good idea!" I grin. I've never met anyone with more good ideas than Maryellen!

When the sun gets low, Mrs. Larkin says it's time for us to leave the beach. So we pack everything up again and drive home, all sandy and salty, hungry and tired. Mrs. Larkin asks us all to wash the sand off our feet at the spigot outside the kitchen door. I'm helping Mikey, who jiggles and giggles as the cold water hits his feet, when the phone rings inside.

"Ellie," says Mrs. Larkin. "It's for you."

*⁑⁎ *Turn to page 124.*

The next morning, the Larkins load their luggage into the car, along with a hamper of food Grandmom has made.

"Good-bye!" Maryellen and I call out and wave as the car pulls away. Grandpop is holding Tom, Grandmom is holding Mikey, and all four are waving. "Good-bye!"

"I love you!" Maryellen calls. I can see that she is sad to leave her grandparents, and it occurs to me that maybe I'm *lucky* that my grandmother lives with my family. I never thought of it that way before.

The station wagon feels almost too spacious, now that there's only Mr. and Mrs. Larkin, Carolyn, Beverly, Maryellen, and me in it. Maryellen gets out her pad and pencils, and I watch for a while as she sketches with impressive ease. In just a few strokes, she can capture a tree or a house, a horse or a haystack.

"I don't know how you do that," I say with admiration.

"Probably the same way you got to know the constellations—practice!" says Maryellen. "I like to doodle; you like to look at the stars. We've got to figure out a way to get you a telescope somehow."

"We'll have to figure out a way to get a lot of money first," I say. "Telescopes are expensive."

"Maybe you could earn the money," says Carolyn.

"Right!" says Maryellen. "You're awfully good with little kids. Maybe you could babysit or be a mother's helper."

"Maybe," I say. But the problem is, the only little kid I know is Daria, the laptop destroyer. Do I want to spend time with *her*?

We drive north and east, out of Georgia and into North Carolina. The names of the towns begin to seem vaguely familiar to me: Franklin, Canton, and Clyde. After we pass Asheville, I sit up straighter, feeling nervous. Could it be? Yes, I know this road. My stomach ties itself in knots as we pass the Cataloochee ski area. This is the road home! Sure enough, a sign says, "Welcome to Cedar Top." We are driving through *my hometown*.

But of course, I quickly remind myself, it's my hometown as it was more than sixty years ago—half a century before I was even born. Out the car window, I see few buildings that I recognize. There's the old school, a church, the public library, and a few houses

that look familiar. But the town is much smaller and sleepier-looking than the Cedar Top I know.

"This is a pretty town," says Mrs. Larkin. "It's only three o'clock, but Dad and I are willing to stop. Shall we spend the night here, girls?"

"I'd like to stop," says Carolyn.

"I'd like to keep going," says Maryellen.

"Me, too," says Beverly.

"How about you, Sophie?" asks Mr. Larkin. "What do you think?"

Good question: What *do* I think? Part of me is very curious to see what life was like in Cedar Top before I was born—even before my mother was born! But part of me thinks that it might be asking for trouble to stay here. Will I betray the fact that I know the town, and confuse the Larkins, who think I'm from New York like my supposed Aunt Betty?

✳ *To say you'd like to drive on through, turn to page 129.*

✳ *To say you'd like to stay in Cedar Top, turn to page 130.*

✳✳✳✳✳✱✳✳✳✳✳

he hands Maryellen the handset part of the phone. The long spiraled cord stretches out the door.

"Hello?" says Maryellen. "It is? *I did?* Oh, thank you! Yes, I will, yes. Thanks again. Bye!" She hands the phone back to her mother and shouts, "I won! I won! I won the contest!"

Maryellen and I hug and jump up and down, and Beverly squeals with delight.

"What contest?" exclaims Mrs. Larkin.

Maryellen stops bouncing long enough to gasp out, "The new plant store in town had a contest to make up a name and a slogan and a logo, and I *won*, and the prize is twenty-five dollars!"

"Twenty-five dollars?" Mrs. Larkin repeats, astounded. "My word!"

"Hey, Ellie," I say. "I bet you can buy a great new girl's bike with that much money. That'll show Wayne!"

"You're right," says Maryellen. "But you know what? I think I'll just keep on riding Davy's hand-me-down bike. *That* will show Wayne I don't care what *he* thinks. I can ride any bike I want to."

"Good for you!" I say.

"But then what'll you use the prize money for?" asks Beverly.

"I'll buy some art supplies," says Maryellen, "and save the rest for college. That's what I *really* want."

When Maryellen says that, it jolts me. I wonder if the time has come for me to go home to see if I can get what *I* really want: peace with Emma, friendship with Gran—and maybe, someday, a telescope. Thanks to Maryellen, I might finally be ready.

*✳✻ *To stay in Daytona Beach with Maryellen, go online to* **beforever.com/endings**

*✳✻ *To go home, turn to page 139.*

✳✱✳✱✻✱✳✱✳

y promise to Maryellen keeps me tossing and turning all night.

The next morning, sad but sure, I tell her, "I've been thinking about what you said last night, about telling Emma the truth. So—" I swallow hard. "Even though I hate to leave, I think I should go home to my family right away."

"Right away?" Maryellen repeats. "You mean, *today*?"

"Yes," I say in a soft voice. "I miss my mom and dad."

Maryellen nods slowly. "I'll hate to see you go," she says. "But I understand why you want to, and I'm glad you're going to stick up for yourself."

She comes with me when I go to Mr. and Mrs. Larkin and Grandpop and Grandmom and she stands next to me as I say, "I think I need to see my family right way. Could you please drop me off at the airport when we leave here? I'll use my return ticket to fly back to my family."

"Oh, Sophie, dear girl, we'll miss you," says Mrs. Larkin. "But if you think that's what you should do, of course we understand."

As the Larkins pack up the car and say their good-
byes and thank-yous, I put my ski-team uniform back
on, fold Carolyn's clothes neatly, and leave them in
the Airstream. When I come out, I hug Grandmom,
Grandpop, and Tom good-bye. I save Mikey for last.
"Bye, Mikey," I say softly.

"Soapy bye?" he says. He looks so sad and confused
that I have to hurry away to the car. I don't want Mikey
to see me cry.

Mr. and Mrs. Larkin, Carolyn, Beverly, Maryellen,
and I get into the car and pull away, waving out the car
windows as we go.

Maryellen and I don't talk much on the way to the
airport, but we hold hands, and we both know what the
other is thinking: *We may be saying good-bye, but I will
never forget you!*

At the airport, Mr. Larkin parks the car and he and
Mrs. Larkin and Maryellen start to get out, but I say,
"No, please, everyone stay in the car. I can handle the
ticket exchange, and I'd like to say good-bye here."

"All right," says Mr. Larkin.

I've been wondering why the watch sent me to
Maryellen, and now I think I know. She has helped me,

*****❄*****

and now it is my turn to help her. "Ellie," I say, through the open car window, "I promised you that I would go home and demand a second chance to tell my story. Will you promise me to go back to the school newspaper and ask for a second chance to tell *your* story, too? Whatever that story may be?"

"I promise," says Maryellen. She sticks out her hand and we shake, sealing the promise.

Mr. Larkin starts the engine. Maryellen leans her head out of the window, and we wave until we cannot see each other anymore. I wish I had a telescope now, so that I could see the car longer.

But it disappears. And when it is out of sight, I click the watch.

*** *Turn to page 136.*

I t would just be too completely weird to stay overnight in Cedar Top, so I say, "If it's okay with you, I'd like to keep on going."

"It's a tie," says Mr. Larkin. "Three votes to stop, three votes to keep going. Since I'm the driver, I'll break the tie and change my vote. Let's go a little farther before we stop."

Phew. I'm relieved.

As we drive through the town, we pass the house my grandmother used to live in before she moved in with us. Wouldn't it be nice if I could become friends with her, the way Maryellen is friends with her grandparents? Maybe I could even make her proud of me, the way Maryellen's grandparents are proud of her. I think of how much fun I had with Tom and Mikey. Maybe it would be fun to make friends with Daria, instead of closing the door in her face. And if I entertained Daria, I'd be helping Gran, and doing her a favor, and that would please her. Maybe—my heart feels both heavy with sadness and light with excitement as I think this— it is time for me to go home and try.

*** *Turn to page 141.*

*****✳*****

I just can't pass up the chance of seeing what Cedar Top was like sixty years ago. Who's ever had such a cool opportunity? Curiosity wins, and I say, "Please, I—I would like to stay here tonight."

"That's fine with me," says Mr. Larkin. "Cedar Top looks like a nice place to spend the night."

I pipe up, "I know this town. My grandmother is from Cedar Top."

"Really? How great!" says Maryellen. "Let's visit her!"

I shake my head. "I'm afraid we can't," I say. "She, uh, moved recently."

Mr. Larkin finds a shady spot to park the trailer overnight, and everyone scatters. Mr. and Mrs. Larkin decide to go grocery shopping. Beverly and Carolyn spot a music store they want to visit; it sells records, sheet music, and even instruments. Maryellen and I want to find a drugstore where we can buy postcards for Grandmom, Grandpop, Tom, and Mikey in Georgia, and Joan and Jerry back in Daytona Beach.

Mr. Larkin unhooks two bicycles from the back end of the trailer. "Here you go, girls," he says. "Sophie, you can ride Carolyn's bike." As I thank him, he wheels

the other bike to Maryellen. It is an old clunker with fat tires, rusty handlebars, a broken bell, and a battered basket. It doesn't look speedy at all. Even so, Maryellen's dad tells her, "Remember to take it easy, sport."

"I will," sighs Maryellen.

"What's the matter?" I ask, after Mr. Larkin has left. "Why did he tell you to take it easy?"

"Three years ago, I had polio," Maryellen says seriously. "It weakened my lungs. My dad doesn't want me to get winded from riding my bike too fast."

I look again at Maryellen's bike, and I guess I look dubious, because she laughs and says, "Yes, my bike is a clunker. And it's really too small for me. I'd love a new one. My friend Davy says that my bike only looks slow until I start to pedal it." She smiles. "I do like to go fast. That's what my dad is worried about."

I grin. "My parents fuss, too. That's what parents do."

"I know," says Maryellen. "But I never let polio slow me down any more than I let this old bike slow me down."

Maryellen's right: She zips along on her fat-tire bike.

Luckily, there aren't very many cars on the quiet streets of Cedar Top, 1955, even when we come to the downtown shopping area. Maryellen and I lean our bikes against a parking meter and go into a store called a "Five and Ten." I wish this store were still in Cedar Top in the twenty-first century! It has gum and candy, toys, birds—real live birds!—magazines, and of course, postcards. Maryellen and I choose two cards. On the back of each, Maryellen writes "We miss you!" and sketches funny cartoons of all of us stuffed in the station wagon, waving out the windows.

Maryellen writes the date on the cards, too, and when I see "November 1955," something tugs at my memory. What does that date mean to me? I wish I could remember!

As Maryellen and I put our cards in a mailbox, I see something bright and shiny on the ground. I pick it up. It's a 1955 penny, brand new.

"Hey, look," I say, holding it in my palm. "Somebody dropped this."

Maryellen squints at it. "There's something wrong with it. See? The date looks funny, as if it were stamped twice." She shrugs. "Oh well, it's still money, and

'finders keepers, losers weepers,' so it's yours now.
Want to buy a gumball with it?"

For a moment, I'm tempted. Then, "No, thanks,"
I say. "I'm not supposed to chew gum." Of course, I'm
not supposed to ride a bike without a helmet or ride in
the car without wearing a seat belt, either. But no one
wears helmets or seat belts here, so I don't really have a
choice about those things. "Besides," I add, "my grandmother collects weird stuff. Maybe she'll get a kick out
of this messed-up penny."

I stick the penny in my pocket. If it makes the
trip back to the twenty-first century with me, it will
be proof that this visit with Maryellen isn't all just a
dream.

We walk awhile, and I find the street that my
grandmother used to live on before she moved in with
us. I'm comforted to see that her old house is there.
"This is the house my grandmother used to live in,"
I tell Maryellen.

"Where does your grandmother live now?" asks
Maryellen.

"Gran lives with us," I say.

"You're lucky!" says Maryellen.

✸✱✸✱✸✹✸✱✸✱✸

"Uh, well, yes, I guess so," I say. "Except it means that I have to share a room with my sister, and neither of us is happy about *that*."

"But you're happy that your Gran lives with you, aren't you?" asks Maryellen.

I shrug.

Maryellen looks puzzled, so I explain. "I don't really know my grandmother very well. She isn't— cozy, like your grandmother. Until she retired, she was always traveling all over the globe, so we hardly ever saw her. Mom says Gran was famous at her job, but I've never talked to Gran about it—or anything else, actually. Even now that she lives in our house, she mostly stays in her room, organizing all the stuff she has collected."

"What stuff?" asks Maryellen.

"It's just a bunch of dusty, old, broken-up things," I say. "She invited my sister and me to come look at her collection, but we didn't do it."

"Why not?" asks Maryellen.

"Because . . ." I hesitate, sort of ashamed to admit it. "I guess because she seems more interested in that old stuff than in us."

Maryellen raises her eyebrows. "If her stuff is *that* interesting, I'd be dying of curiosity to see it!"

I grin. Maryellen has a point. When I go home, I'll ask Gran about her stuff, instead of resenting it.

Maryellen and I are about to pedal away from Gran's old house when *boom!* The front door bursts open and a boy flies out, takes the steps in a running leap, and runs down the sidewalk.

"Stop him!" shouts a girl about our age who comes bounding out the door right after the boy. "He took it!"

*** Turn to page 143.

****

I'm back on the ski-race awards platform. I turn to Coach Stanislav and say, "I didn't cheat—I made a mistake. Please give me a second chance to explain."

Coach Stanislav hesitates, but suddenly, Emma speaks up. "I made a mistake, too," she says. "I saw Sophie take the shortcut, and I jumped to a conclusion. I don't know what happened, but I do know Sophie, and she would never cheat. She deserves a chance to explain, Coach."

"All right," says Coach Stanislav. He takes off his sunglasses and looks at me eye-to-eye. "Sophie, tell us again—slowly and clearly—what happened."

I take a deep breath, and explain. When I'm finished, Coach Stanislav says, "I'm sorry we accused you of cheating. I'm glad you had a second chance to explain."

Emma hugs me. "Will you give *me* a second chance, Sophie?" she asks. "I should never have distrusted you."

Mom and Dad are beaming, and my heart is full of happiness. I give Emma a Larkin-style hug, one that is big and exuberant and full of affection. Part of me that had been missing has been found again.

✳

Later, when we're home in our room, Emma says,
"I hope we never have a misunderstanding like that
again." She runs to her dresser drawer and pulls out
some goggles. "Take these," she says. "They're new.
They're tinted, so I think they'll help you when you ski
in bright sunlight. You can wear them in our next race."

She tries to hand me the goggles, but I shake my
head. "No thanks, Em." I take a deep breath. Telling
Emma how I feel about ski team is as hard as speaking
up on the ski-awards platform was. "There isn't going
to be another race for me. Being on the team is good for
you, but not for me. I only joined because I thought it
would make you happy."

"But doesn't skiing make you happy?"

"I love skiing," I say. That is, I love to be outside in
the cold, snowy air, swooping along in the quiet white-
ness, smelling the pines, flying over the snow just for
the joy of it. "But I want to ski for fun from now on."

Emma shakes her head, as if she can't quite understand what she's hearing. "So all this time, you've been
skiing on the team only because you thought I wanted
you to?"

"Yes. But now I know that that was wrong, for me

*****❄*****

and for you." I think of how Maryellen yearned to stand out in her family, and I tell Emma, "We're twins, but we're different people, and we should each do the things we love."

We're quiet for a moment. Finally Emma says, "You're positive you want to quit?"

"I'm sure."

"All right, then." Emma sighs. Then she slips me a crooked, mischievous grin. "I kind of guessed that you didn't like the uniform. You always groaned every time you pulled it on." She moans, pretending to be me.

I laugh. "I hate the uniforms most of all!" I say, tossing a pillow at her.

She tosses it right back. "Then can I have yours?"

"You mean *may* you have mine, and yes, you may," I say. "No backsies."

"You bet!" says Emma, and I smile. When she says that, she reminds me of Maryellen!

❋ *The End* ❋

*To read this story another way and see how different choices
lead to a different ending, turn back to page 116.*

❋∗❋✳❋∗❋

hen the little kids finish washing the sand off their feet, they go inside the house. Maryellen's about to go inside, too, but I take her arm and hold her back so that we're both in the shade cast by the trailer.

"Ellie—" I stop. Maryellen's looking at me with such joy, I can't bear to make her sad! But I force myself to continue. "I—I'm going home now."

"Okay!" says Maryellen lightly. "See you tomorrow."

"No," I say slowly. "I don't think so. What I mean is, my family and I will be in Cedar Top for Thanksgiving." Then I add, "And, Ellie, if we don't end up moving here, I won't see you again."

"Wait—*what*?" asks Maryellen. She frowns as if she's struggling to understand what I've said. "Never again? That's terrible! We've had so much fun. We're such good friends!"

"We'll always be good friends, because we'll always remember each other," I assure her. "But now I have to say good-bye."

Maryellen doesn't talk. She hugs me instead. "Good-bye, Sophie," she says at last. She gives me another quick hug and then hurries inside the house, as if she's afraid she'll cry if she stays a second longer.

I take a shaky breath and go into the trailer. I change out of Carolyn's bathing suit and hang it in the tiny bathroom. My ski uniform feels tight when I pull it on. Then I click the stopwatch.

*** *Turn to page 173.*

The road we're on is mountainous and twisty. Soon Cedar Top has disappeared, left behind around a curve. I'm thinking hard, trying to come up with a way to leave the Larkins without worrying them. I put on my ski-team uniform this morning, so I'll be ready to go when the time comes.

Mrs. Larkin is looking at the map. "Asheville is a big town," she says. "We can spend the night there."

I'm pretty sure there's an airport in Asheville. I take a deep breath and say, "I'm really sorry, but I think I should go home to my family."

"Oh, Sophie!" Maryellen exclaims. "Why?"

"I miss them," I say simply. "I've loved being with you, Ellie. But now it's time for me to go. Mr. Larkin, may I ask you to drop me off at the Asheville airport? I'll use my—um—return ticket to get home. Then I can see my family right away."

Maryellen takes my hand in both of hers and squeezes it.

"Well, Sophie," says Mrs. Larkin, "we'll hate to say good-bye to you, but if you think that's what you should do . . ."

"Yes," I say unhappily but firmly, "I do."

✳✳✳✳✳✲✳✳✳✳✳

"Then yes, of course, I'll drive you to the airport,"
says Mr. Larkin. "It's on our route."

∗

All too soon, we arrive at the airport. Mr. Larkin
pulls up to the curb, and everyone gets out of the car.
I hug Carolyn and Beverly, Mr. and Mrs. Larkin, and,
last of all, Maryellen. "Thank you so much, all of you,"
I say. "I feel as though I have two families to love now:
my own and yours."

Maryellen hugs me again, saying, "I'll miss you,
Sophie."

"I'll miss you, too," I reply. "I'll never forget you."

Mr. Larkin starts to lead me into the airport, but I
tell him, "Thank you, but I can handle this myself. I'd
rather say good-bye to all of you out here."

As the Larkins get back in the station wagon,
I wave, and Maryellen waves back to me until the
Airstream is just a silver dot. When it disappears
completely, I click the stopwatch button.

∗∗ *Turn to page 155.*

∗∗∗∗✳∗∗∗∗

e don't need to be asked twice. Maryellen pedals so quickly that she's a blur. I'm close behind her, and the other girl is running behind me yelling, "Stop, Roy! You give that back!"

Maryellen catches up with the boy and, like a daredevil, swerves her bike in front of him so that he has to stop. Instead, *bam!* The boy knocks Maryellen down. He falls, too, and is soon tangled up in the bike, which skids sideways until, *slam!* It smashes into a tree. Maryellen grabs the boy by one arm. With the other arm, he tosses something into the grass.

The girl and I catch up just as the boy disentangles himself and runs away down the street. "You'll never find it!" he taunts the girl as he runs off.

"Are you all right?" the girl asks Maryellen, helping her get up.

"I'm fine," says Maryellen, out of breath. She dusts off her hands, which are scraped and dirty from her fall.

I've dropped my bike and I'm on my hands and knees searching the grass where I saw the object land. "Is this what you lost?" I ask the girl. I hold up a small, sharp rock that has been shaped into a point.

⁕⁕⁕⁕✲⁕⁕⁕

"Yes, oh *yes*," she says, elated. "Oh, thank you both so much."

I give it to her. "It's an arrowhead, right?"

She nods. "I found it in the woods. I've found other ones there before, but this is the best specimen I've ever dug up. I brought it home to clean it off, and then my brother grabbed it and ran. I would have lost it for sure if not for you two." She smiles. "My name is Nancy, by the way. Leave your bike and come with me so we can wash off your hands," she says to Maryellen.

"I'm Sophie," I say. "And this is Ellie."

"Nice to meet you, Sophie and Ellie," says Nancy. "Well, I mean, I'm *glad* to meet you, even if the way we met wasn't so nice."

"Talk about beginning a friendship with a bang!" jokes Maryellen, which makes us laugh together as if we're old friends.

Nancy leads us to her house. I feel a little weird, knowing that this is the house my grandmother once lived in. I only visited her here a few times when I was little, but I remember that she had lots of books everywhere. Nancy's family is tidier; the house is spick-and-span. Nancy shows us her collection of arrowheads. "How did you know this is an arrowhead?" she asks me.

"My grandmother collects them. She studies how people lived a long time ago. She goes to places where Native Americans and early settlers lived and digs things up, like broken bits of old pots and stuff."

"You mean your grandmother's an *archaeologist*?" asks Nancy, sounding impressed.

"Mm-hmm," I say. I've never thought of it as a big deal.

"Golly," says Nancy. "That's fantastic, Sophie! How did she ever get to be an archaeologist? I know it's awfully hard to do, because, well . . ." Nancy sounds wistful. "*I* want to be an archaeologist, too, when I grow up, but—"

"Huh!" Just then, annoying Roy sticks his head into Nancy's room. He scoffs, "How many times have I told you? Girls are mothers or teachers or nurses or secretaries. Girls can't be scientists."

"Yes, they can!" Maryellen and I state staunchly.

Roy leans against the door frame and sneers, "Oh yeah? Who's ever heard of a lady archaeologist? Name one."

"Sophie's grandmother," Maryellen and Nancy say triumphantly, pointing to me.

"Oh," says Roy, genuinely surprised. It is very satisfying to see him so deflated.

"Get lost, Roy," says Nancy.

"Dumb girls," Roy mutters as he slinks off.

We three girls share a conspiratorial smile. Nancy says, "Please thank your grandmother for me, Sophie. Tell her she's given me hope."

"Yes," Maryellen says, "your grandmother must be an unusual person."

I nod. I don't want to admit that I've never bothered to ask Gran about her work. It never occurred to me that she was unusual, or that she had to push against ideas of what girls could or could not do. I've always taken it for granted that I can be anything I want to be when I grow up. Clearly, it was not the same for girls in the 1950s.

When I get home, I think I'll ask Gran to tell me how she became an archaeologist. I wonder if there were people along the way who told her that she couldn't, and if so, how she had the courage to ignore them.

❋

When we go back outside, Nancy says, "I'm afraid you're going to need a new bike, Ellie."

We all look at Maryellen's bike, dismayed. The front tire is bent out of shape so that it wobbles wildly. The seat is knocked sideways, and the handlebars are cockeyed.

"It wasn't that great a bike to begin with," says Maryellen. "Now it's *really* hopeless."

I say comfortingly, "Pretty soon you'll be tall enough to ride Carolyn's bike. I'm sure she'll hand it down to you when she outgrows it."

"I already have another bike at home," Maryellen says. "My friend Davy gave me his when he outgrew it and got a new one. But . . . " She pauses.

"But what?" Nancy asks.

"Well, it's a boy's bike," says Maryellen. "It has a bar across the middle."

"So?" I ask.

"So I'm afraid my friends will tease me. They'll say girls don't ride boys' bikes," Maryellen admits sheepishly.

"Be like Sophie's grandmother," says Nancy. "Don't worry about what *other* people say girls can and can't do."

"Yes," I agree. "If Nancy can be an archaeologist, then you can ride a boy's bike, for Pete's sake! Besides, you pedal so fast that no one will see the bike anyway," I joke. "It'll just look like a streak."

Maryellen laughs.

"Promise me that when you get back home you'll ride that bike," I say.

"I promise," says Maryellen. "And if people tease me about it, I'll just challenge them to a race."

Nancy holds out the arrowhead. "Let's promise on the arrowhead that we'll all be who we want to be, and do what we want to do, no matter what anyone says to discourage us."

Maryellen and I put our hands on top of the arrowhead, and we all say, "I promise!"

Then Maryellen and I say good-bye to Nancy and wheel our bikes away. Maryellen does the best she can with her wreck of a bike. We turn to wave one last time when we get to the corner and Nancy calls out, "I will never forget you two—or your grandmother, Sophie!"

My grandmother. I feel my heartbeat quicken with

urgency. I don't want to leave Maryellen, but I *do* want to go home and get to know Gran.

∗∗∗ *To stay with Maryellen,*
turn to page 150.

∗∗∗ *To go home,*
turn to page 158.

∗∗∗∗∗✳∗∗∗∗

ut not yet. I'm not quite ready to go back to the deep freeze of unhappiness and accusation on the ski-race awards platform, and I want to stay with Maryellen until we get to Washington, D.C.

Still, the next day, as we get closer and closer, I get nervous. The Larkins believe that they are driving me home to my family's new house. But of course, I have no family in Washington, D.C. and no house, new *or* old. What am I going to say when they ask me what my new address is? I glue my nose to the car window, as if the answer to my problem is out there.

"Are you excited about seeing your family soon?" Maryellen asks me.

I nod, managing a weak smile.

"There are so many famous places in Washington, D.C.," says Maryellen. "What do you want to see first? The Lincoln Memorial? The Smithsonian?"

"Well," I say, "those all sound great, but most of all I want to go to the Naval Observatory." The truth is that the Naval Observatory is the *only* place I know about in D.C., because they have huge telescopes there that track the planets and stars. Ever since I was a little kid, I've been fascinated by the night sky. Last summer, I

wanted to go to astronomy camp, but Emma didn't, so I gave in as usual and went to ski-training camp instead.

"What would you do at the Naval Observatory?" Maryellen asks.

"I've always dreamed of looking through one of the huge telescopes to see the moon and stars up close. I get shivers thinking about it!" I say. "I'd also like to see the clock that's the official timekeeper of the United States." I glance down at the watch on my wrist with a secret grin. I bet the people at the observatory would get shivers if they knew what *my* watch can do. It not only keeps time, it sent me *traveling back* in time, too. The clock at the Naval Observatory can't do that!

"Let's find the Naval Observatory on this map," says Maryellen, unfolding a big paper map of Washington, D.C. on her lap.

I squint at the maze of lines and labels. I have no idea how to use it. I'd have more luck navigating by the stars the way ancient travelers did than I would using a paper map! But of course, GPS and smartphones haven't been invented yet in 1955. So I watch closely as Maryellen finds "Naval Observatory, H4" on the map's list of place names. Then, tracing with her finger, she

finds where the line labeled H crosses the line labeled 4 on the map. "Here it is," she says. And sure enough, there's a dot labeled in tiny letters, "Naval Observatory, 3450 Massachusetts Avenue NW."

"I like how maps just use dots and lines to show you a place," says Maryellen.

"Sort of like your doodles do," I point out.

"You sounded like a rooster!" says Beverly, and we laugh.

Maryellen shows me how to use the map to follow the route to Mr. Larkin's friend Dave Blanchard's house. We look at street signs, and then find those streets on the map. Maryellen tells her dad when to turn left or right, and how many more blocks to go before he does, and soon we're pulling into Mr. Blanchard's driveway. The plan is for us to park the trailer here and spend the night. Then the Larkins will deliver me to my family tomorrow.

Dave Blanchard is a hearty, jolly guy who seems very pleased to have the trailer in his driveway. He and Mr. Larkin disconnect the trailer from the car. Then, as a thank-you, Mr. Blanchard takes us all out to dinner.

After dinner, Mr. Larkin announces a surprise.

"Girls, tonight we're going to the National Theater to see . . ." He pauses and looks at Beverly, and then says dramatically, "a ballet!"

Beverly is speechless. She sits on the edge of her seat in the car, and when we get to the theater and the ballet begins, she sits on the edge of her seat there, too. She's not so much seeing the ballet as *consuming* it.

Maryellen nudges me, nods at Beverly, and whispers, "She's wishing she had her tutu, so she could pirouette her way up to the stage and dance with the ballerinas."

Carolyn, as enraptured by the music as Beverly is by the dancers, seems hardly to be breathing, and her fingers move on an invisible keyboard hovering above her lap. It's really wonderful to see both Beverly and Carolyn so intently absorbed. It is as if they have been transported into another world just the way the watch transported me, but in their cases, it is ballet and music that have worked the magic.

*

That night, when Maryellen and I settle in for our last night in the trailer, she sighs.

****

"What's the matter?" I ask.

"This is our last night together," she says sadly. "I wish we could have more time."

"Me too," I agree.

"Hey, Sophie," says Maryellen, perky as she always is when her popcorn popper of a brain comes up with a great idea. "Listen! Your family thinks you're flying here, right? When do they expect you?"

"Uh, tomorrow night, I guess," I say.

"Then there's no reason why we have to take you home first thing in the morning," says Maryellen. "Let's ask Mom and Dad if we can all have one last day together, and we'll drive you home tomorrow evening."

"I love that idea," I say. And I do love it—not only because it will give me more time to figure out how to part from the Larkins, but because it will give me more time with Maryellen.

✳✱ Turn to page 160.

✳✱✳✱✳✱✳✱

woosh! For a second, I have the sensation that I'm flying and then . . . I open my eyes and I'm on the ski-race awards platform, surrounded by frowns and worried looks.

"I didn't win the race," I say as I hand the watch back to the judge. "But I didn't cheat, either." I explain what happened quickly, clearly, and decisively.

The judge shakes my hand. "Thank you for telling us the facts," she says. "I can see that you made an honest mistake."

I'm so relieved that I have that flying feeling the watch gave me. It feels great to have my record clear with the judge, Coach Stanislav, my team, my parents and Gran, and most of all, Emma.

Later, at home, Emma says, "I'm sorry I accused you of cheating, Sophie. Can you forgive me?"

"Yes," I say, hugging her. "And speaking of forgiving, I think you and I should forgive Daria. She's just a little kid; she didn't mean to break your laptop."

"I suppose not," says Emma uncertainly.

"Come on," I urge. "Let's go talk to her. She and her mom are with Gran."

We go down the hall. When we enter Gran's room,

she and Daria's mother look up from the box of bones they are sorting. Daria looks up from drawing.

"May we borrow Daria?" I ask. "Emma and I have something fun to do, and we think Daria would like it, too."

"That would be great," says Gran. She sounds pleased, which pleases me.

"Come on, Daria," I say.

"Okay!" she says, smiling at me. I never noticed before how her smile lights up her whole face. Well, of course—I guess I never saw her smile before! I take her by the hand; it's little, and it reminds me of Mikey's plump hand. Emma follows us to the bathroom. I fill the sink with soapsuds, pat some onto my face, and say,

I'll pretend to shave my face,
Then Daria can take my place
And I'll make up a funny poem
Like one of Burma Shave's—
You know 'em?

Pretty soon we're all laughing so loud that Gran and Daria's mom come to see what we're up to. When

they see our soapy beards, they laugh, too. And they laugh even harder when, inspired by Mikey, I say, "Just call me Soapy Sophie."

Gran hugs me, and I can tell that we're going to be good friends from now on. I'm even more sure when Gran catches my eye in the mirror and winks as if to say, "Nice work, Sophie." I think she's even a little proud of me!

✳ *The End* ✳

To read this story another way and see how different choices lead to a different ending, turn back to page 123.

✳✳*✳✳✳*✳*✳*

That night, when Maryellen and I are snuggled into our sleeping bags in the trailer, I say, "You know what, Ellie? I've been thinking about my grandmother. I haven't been fair to her. I think . . . well, I think I should go home and try to get to know her and make things right with her."

"Home?" says Maryellen. "When?"

"I think I had better leave tomorrow," I say.

"I was afraid you were going to say that." She sighs heavily. Then she adds, "But I understand."

"I knew you would." I can't say more; my heart is too full.

*

The next morning, I put my ski uniform back on. I slide the penny deep into my pocket, wondering if it will be transported back with me.

Maryellen and I explain to Mr. and Mrs. Larkin, and though they are sorry, they agree that I should go. While Mr. Larkin detaches the Airstream from the car, I hug Beverly, thank Carolyn for the loan of her clothes, and kiss Mrs. Larkin good-bye. Then Maryellen and I climb into the car. I wave to Mrs. Larkin and the girls,

standing in front of the Airstream, and they wave back. Maryellen and I sit close to each other, so in tune with our thoughts that we don't need to speak, while Mr. Larkin drives to the nearest airport, which is a few miles west of Cedar Top.

When we get there, I say, "Thanks for everything, Mr. Larkin. Your family taught me how good it feels to be welcome and included. I can handle changing my ticket, and if it's okay, I'd rather say good-bye out here."

"All right, Sophie," says Mr. Larkin. He shakes my hand. "It's been a pleasure. Never forget that you're an honorary Larkin."

"I won't!" I promise. "Good-bye."

Maryellen hugs me and whispers, "Remember the arrowhead promise."

"I will," I say fervently. "You, too."

"I will," says Maryellen, and I know she means it with all her heart. Slowly, she gets back into the car. She waves out the car window as Mr. Larkin drives away.

I wave, too, until I can't see Maryellen anymore. Then I press the button on the watch.

✻ Turn to page 165.

✻✻*✻❋✻*✻*✻*

aryellen presents her brainstorm to Mr. and Mrs. Larkin the next morning, and they are as happy as we are with the plan to keep me with them all day. We drive the car, which feels very zippy now without the trailer attached, into the heart of Washington, D.C. We park and set forth on foot. Maryellen uses her map skills to lead us from the Lincoln Memorial to the Washington Monument to the Capitol to the Library of Congress. After lunch, we go to the National Gallery.

"My feet are tired," Beverly complains after we've looked at a few rooms full of sculptures.

"*Your* feet?" Mr. Larkin teases gently. "Your bouncy little feet that can do ballet for hours on end? They're *tired*?"

"They're tired of this museum," says Beverly. "And also, I'm thirsty."

"I tell you what," says Mrs. Larkin. "I'll take Beverly to the museum restaurant while the rest of you tour the museum. We'll meet in the restaurant at three."

Mr. Larkin nods. "I could use a cup of coffee too, so I'll come with you and Beverly. Carolyn, Ellie, and Sophie will be all right on their own for a while."

"See you at three!" Carolyn says gaily as she and

Maryellen and I take off together. As we enter the section of the museum that has paintings, Maryellen stops still. On her face is an expression of awe.

"What?" I ask.

"These paintings are famous," she says reverently. "I mean, they are by the greatest artists who have ever lived, like Leonardo da Vinci and Vermeer and Van Gogh. I've seen photos of some of these paintings in books, but it's amazing to see them in real life."

She stands and stares at every painting, almost as if she is walking into it, as if she wants to examine every brushstroke to see how the painter created such beauty. She moves so slowly that Carolyn and I get ahead of her and have to go back to look for her.

We find her in a room full of modern paintings. The paintings are colorful and weird. Splotches of color and crazy shapes are splashed across the canvases.

"I get really excited when I see paintings like these," says Maryellen. "Some artists paint people and landscapes the way they really look—their paintings are amazingly realistic. But other artists, like these, paint with wild imagination, so that their people and scenes look like something in a dream."

"You can say that again," says Carolyn. "Some of them hardly even look like art. They're strange."

"The museum signs say that some of these artists were criticized at first for being different or painting pictures people thought were strange," says Maryellen. "But now their pictures are hanging *here*, in a grand museum, admired by millions of people. So I guess art doesn't have to be just one certain way. There are lots of different ways of seeing things, and showing things, and doing things." She pauses. "And that's true about life, too."

I see Maryellen's sketch pad and notice that with her usual remarkable talent for doodling, she has captured some of the paintings in just a few lines.

"I don't know how you do it. You draw just the bare bones, and somehow, your sketches help me see the paintings more clearly. Hey, you know what, Ellie?" I say. "When you go back to school, I think that you should ask if you can be the *cartoonist* for the school newspaper, not a writer."

"The *cartoonist*?" ask Maryellen and Carolyn together.

"Yes," I say, exuberantly, the way Maryellen talks

when she has a great idea. "Trust me, kids will like your funny sketch of a cow better than an essay about milk."

Maryellen looks doubtful. "But my doodles are—"

"—brilliant," I interrupt. "They're quirky and goofy and smart, just like you."

"That's true. No one else draws quite the way you do," says Carolyn.

"Will they take me seriously as an artist, though?" asks Maryellen.

"They will if you take *yourself* seriously," I say. "Promise you will."

Maryellen hugs me, then steps back and grins. She says, "I promise."

"It's nearly three o'clock," says Carolyn. "We'd better go to the restaurant to meet the rest of the family."

We wend our way through the halls of the museum, and when we get to the restaurant, Mrs. Larkin says, "Hi, girls. I bought some postcards of the White House. Would you like to send one to Grandmom and Grandpop?"

"Yes, thanks," says Maryellen. She takes one and writes the date on the top of the postcard.

****

I get that familiar funny feeling when I read it: Tuesday, November 29, 1955.

Why is that date significant to me? It's driving me crazy! I know that something important happened on this day. But what?

** Turn to page 169.

woosh. . .

I'm back on the ski-race awards platform with the judge and Coach Stanislav glaring at me. I spot my grandmother standing next to my parents. Handing the watch to the judge, I say, "I don't deserve this watch, because I didn't win the race. But I don't deserve to be called a cheater, either." Then I step off the platform and go to my grandmother, and I say, "Please help me, Gran. You had to stand up for yourself to become an archaeologist. Will you help me stand up for myself now?"

Gran smiles, her bright blue eyes sparkling. "Of course I will," she says, and we walk back to the platform together.

It's wonderful how Gran puts her scientific archaeologist's mind to work and says, "We'll find evidence that Sophie didn't cheat."

The coach, the judge, my grandmother, and I go back to the place where the trail split. Gran points out that the flag marking the correct branch has fallen over and is buried in the snow. We also find ski marks in the snow which show that someone was standing there recently—probably the person who directed me to the

wrong branch of the trail by mistake. Gran also points out that because of the glare on the snow, it would have been very hard for me to see, especially when I was skiing fast.

Gran is brisk and decisive; no one argues with her facts. Because of her help, my name is cleared. I have never felt so relieved in my life!

*

"Thank you, Gran," I say. It's later, and we're home in my—no, in Gran's—room. I take the 1955 penny out of my pocket. "I thought you might be interested in this penny that I found," I say, handing it to her.

"Hmmm," says Gran. She gets out her magnifying glass, and while she inspects the penny, I spot an arrowhead on her desk.

"Where did you find this arrowhead?" I ask.

"I found it in the woods near my house when I was a young girl," says Gran. "It's very special to me. I almost lost it the day I found it, but a friend rescued it for me. Her name was Sophie, and that's why I suggested that your parents name *you* Sophie. I've always kept that arrowhead near me, because I made

a promise on it. I promised that I would be an archaeologist. That promise changed my life."

Wait, what? I'm dumbfounded. Could it be? Are Gran and Nancy the same person? Am I the Sophie she met, the one who found her arrowhead?

I begin to sputter, but before I can speak, Gran hands the penny back to me and says with a mysterious smile, "This penny is going to change your life."

"It is?" I whisper. "How?"

"That is a 1955 double-die wheat penny," Gran says. "It is very rare and valuable, because the mint accidentally double-printed the date on it." She looks at me over the top of her eyeglasses. "Is there anything you have your heart set on?" she asks.

"A telescope," I say immediately.

"Ah! You are a fellow scientist," says Gran, pleased. "Well, your penny is worth nearly two thousand dollars. I think you can buy a fine telescope with that—and still have some to put away for your college education."

"Wow," I breathe, looking at the penny in the palm of my hand. I'm thinking, *Hey, Ellie, guess what? Turns out it's a good thing I didn't buy that gumball!* I smile at

Gran and ask, "Will you help me sell the penny and choose a telescope?"

"I'd be glad to," says Gran. "That's just the kind of project I love." She clicks on her laptop and then puts her arm around me and pulls me close so that I can see the screen, too. "Let's begin," she says.

∗ The End ∗

To read this story another way and see how different choices lead to a different ending, turn back to page 149.

uddenly, I remember what happened on that date. And suddenly, I know how to say goodbye to the Larkins *and* the perfect way to thank them, both at the same time.

I'm so excited that I can hardly sit still when we're back in the car. Everyone else has long faces, and Maryellen holds my hand as if she can't bear the thought of parting from me.

"Well, Soapy Sophie," says Mr. Larkin mournfully, "I'm afraid we can't put it off any longer. It's time for me to give you a ride home. What's your address?"

"Please drive to 3450 Massachusetts Avenue, Northwest," I say.

We don't have to go very far. When we pull up to the huge marble building with the sky-high roof, Mr. Larkin says, "This can't be right. Sophie, kiddo, are you sure of that address?"

"Is this your house?" asks Beverly, wide-eyed.

"No," I admit. "This is the Naval Observatory. I wanted you all to come here today because I want to thank you for taking me on this trip with you. Come with me."

The Larkins look puzzled, but Mr. Larkin parks the

car and they all follow me into the observatory.

"Why are we here?" asks Carolyn.

I smile, happy to tell the wonderful thing that I remembered. "There is a total lunar eclipse today," I announce. "And it's a full moon. The moon is below the horizon here in Washington, D.C., so we can't see it in the sky—but here at the observatory, we can see what the eclipse looks like in the planetarium star show!"

"Neato!" says Maryellen.

"What a great idea," says Mrs. Larkin.

"And a *heavenly* surprise," jokes Mr. Larkin. "I guess when it comes to Sophie and good ideas, the sky's the limit."

We laugh and groan at his joke, and then Carolyn says, "But seriously, Sophie. How did you know about the eclipse?"

"Oh, Sophie knows everything on earth about the sun, moon, stars, and planets," says Maryellen. "She loves the night sky the way I love sketching. I just know that she'll grow up to be an astronomer."

I grin. "Sounds good to me!"

We go into the planetarium. I get goose bumps when I lean back in my seat and look up at the starry sky on

the dome. It's so beautiful and so *huge*. Maryellen pokes me and points up to the Big Dipper. I know that just as I am, she's remembering that night at her grandparents' house when we first looked at the constellations together. I squeeze her hand, and we watch the lunar eclipse in rapt silence. It is one of the coolest things I've ever seen. As the earth's shadow slips slowly across the moon, I think about how the universe is full of mysteries and miracles, and how lucky I am because I've had my own mysterious and miraculous experience—my time-travel visit to Maryellen.

When the eclipse show is over, I excuse myself, go into the ladies' room, and change back into my ski-team uniform. I rejoin the Larkins and give Carolyn her clothes. Then I tell them, "If you don't mind, I'd like to say good-bye now. I can find my way home from here. I think that would be best."

"Well, all right, dear," says Mrs. Larkin. "If you are sure you can get home—"

"Oh, yes," I say. "I'm sure. I know exactly how to get home." I hug her, and Beverly, and Carolyn, and Mr. Larkin. "Thank you all so much. You'll never know how you've changed my life, and how you've changed *me.* I'll never forget you."

"We'll never forget you, either," says Mr. Larkin.

I hug Maryellen last of all, and she says the best good-bye of all: "I'll think of you every time I look up at the stars, Sophie. Promise you'll think of me when you do, too."

"I promise," I say. "Good-bye."

"Good-bye," says Maryellen.

And then, even though it is the hardest thing I have ever done, I walk away.

✱✲ Turn to page 179.

woosh. . .

I'm back on the ski-race awards platform. No one has moved or blinked an eye or taken a breath since I left.

Everyone is looking at me. Their expressions haven't changed. But *I* have changed: Because of my time with Maryellen, I know now that I can face things that I'm afraid of. Even though I'm still scared to confront the judge and Coach Stanislav, I remember how I felt when I walked into the ocean: I was scared, but I didn't let that stop me. Now, looking at my family, my coach, and the judge, I say, "Listen, please. I will explain what happened in the race."

Only my parents and Gran seem to be listening. Disappointment chills me like a trickle of icy cold water running down my back. But then I think about how Maryellen bravely overcame her fear of speaking, and that gives me courage to speak up. Louder this time, I say, "Please listen to me. Emma is right. I did not win the race."

Emma starts to speak, but I hold up my hand and say, "No, Emma, I can speak for myself." I give the watch back to the judge and repeat, "I didn't win, but

I didn't cheat, either. I made a mistake. Will you come with me back up the mountain, and let me show you where I made my mistake, and why?"

I hold my breath and only exhale after the judge says, "We'll all come."

They do.

After everyone has seen that the flag marking the trail is buried in snow and that there are ski tracks showing that someone was standing right where I said he'd been, pointing me in the wrong direction by mistake, the judge says, "Sophie, we owe you an apology. You were telling the truth. You're disqualified, but we'll clear your name."

"Thank you, ma'am," I say gratefully.

✶

Later, at home, I'm lying on my bed, looking at the stars I've put onto the ceiling, wondering how to make my peace with Emma, when she pokes her head in the door and says, "Can I come in?"

"Sure," I say. "It's your room."

"No, it's *our* room," Emma corrects me as she sits on her bed. "But I'm afraid I haven't made you feel very

welcome in it. I—well, I was mad that we had to share, so I took it out on you, even though it's not your fault. You had to give up your room, too. I'm sorry."

"That's okay," I tell her. I think about Maryellen's room with three girls and a stout old dog in it. "Sharing a room is tricky."

Emma says, "Listen, Sophie. I'm sorry that I said that you cheated. I—I thought maybe you took the shortcut on purpose, so that you could win. I thought you'd want to beat me, because you were mad at me for being mean about the room."

"I haven't been great about sharing the room either." I grin ruefully. "I've been sort of a space invader, haven't I?"

"A what?" asks Emma, with a hint of a smile.

"Well, I mean, I moved into your room and brought all my stuff so that you are squashed. I even put these stars up without asking you," I say.

"Yeah," says Emma. "I guess I just don't get what's so cool about stars."

I think about how everybody in Maryellen's class loved the star show, and I realize that I've never talked to Emma about the stars. Maybe she'll understand why

I want a telescope, and why I want to go to astronomy camp and not ski-training camp next summer, if I can just show her why I love the night sky.

"Hit the lights," I say, and as she flips the switch, the ceiling of our room turns into a starry sky. "See, that group of seven stars right above you is called the Little Dipper, and that group over by the door is called the Big Dipper . . ."

"Oh, because they're shaped like cups with handles!" says Emma. "I get it! This is fun."

"You know who else might think it's fun?" I ask. "Daria."

Emma groans. "Daria the laptop destroyer?"

"I think it's time for us to forgive her for that," I say. "Come on."

Emma stands behind me as I knock on Gran's door.

"Come in," Gran says. She and Daria's mother look up from their work, and Daria looks up from a picture book she's holding.

"Emma and I were wondering if Daria would like to come to our room," I say. "We're putting on a star show."

"Oh?" says Gran, sounding surprised. She turns to

Daria. "Would you like to see Sophie's stars?"

"Yes!" says Daria.

Her mom says it's okay, so I take Daria's hand, and we walk together down the hall.

"*Oooh,*" Daria sighs in awe when she sees the ceiling of stars. She sits on the floor with Emma and me, and I tell them both some of the stories behind the constellations. Then we make up our own stories, which Emma turns out to be great at, and we have so much fun that we're surprised when Gran and Daria's mother come to tell us it's time for Daria to go home.

After Daria and her mom leave, Gran says, "Thank you, girls. It was nice of you to include Daria. She clearly liked it, and her mother and I got a lot done."

"It was all Sophie's idea," says Emma.

Gran smiles at me over the top of her glasses. "It was a good one."

"Gran," I say, "I have another idea I'd like to talk to you about. I'd like to earn money to buy a telescope. May I babysit for Daria when she comes here with her mother?"

"If her mother agrees, we'll give it a try the next time Daria comes," says Gran. "If it goes well, we'll make it a regular job, and I'll pay you three dollars an hour. Does that sound fair?"

"You bet!" I say, echoing Maryellen.

Gran smiles. My heart lifts—she actually looks proud of me. "You're very enterprising, Sophie," she says. "You're sure to get the telescope that you want."

"Then you'll look at the *real* stars," jokes Emma, "just when I've started to like the glow-in-the-dark ones on the ceiling of our room!"

"Oh, they'll stay where they are for a while," I reassure her. "It will take a long time to earn enough money for a telescope."

But I know that Gran is right: I *will* earn enough money eventually, I'm sure. And I'm also sure that whenever I look through my telescope, I'll think of Maryellen, far away in time and space, but never far from my mind and heart.

✲ The End ✲

To read this story another way and see how different choices lead to a different ending, turn back to page 11.

I click the stopwatch, and *swoosh*, I'm swept up in a dizzy whirl. When I open my eyes, I'm back on the ski-race awards platform. Not one second has passed since I first left. I hand the watch back to the judge and I say, "I did *not* cheat. I made a mistake. Please listen while I explain."

＊

Later, at home, when Emma and I are alone, I tell her, "I'm really glad the misunderstanding about the race is cleared up."

"Oh, me, too!" says Emma. "I'm so sorry that I doubted you. I should have known that you would never cheat."

"Well, I may not have cheated in the ski race. But I have been dishonest—with myself and with you."

"What do you mean?" asks Emma.

"Being on the ski team is *your* passion, Emma, not mine," I say.

"Are you—are you quitting the team?" she asks.

"I'll finish the season," I tell her. "But next winter, I'll only ski for fun. No more uniform, no more team, no more Coach Stanislav, no more races."

"But you're so good at skiing," she says. "I thought you loved skiing fast, flying over moguls and going airborne."

"I do," I say, "but not in races. Competition takes all the fun out of it for me."

"Not me! I love to win," says Emma. "I guess you're right, Sophie. Ski team is *my* passion." She looks at me earnestly. "What's yours?"

"Stars," I say. I think of Maryellen, and the starry sky that we saw together, and the wonderful show at the planetarium. "Next summer, I'm going to astronomy camp, not ski camp. What I really want to do most is to look at the stars. *That's* what I love."

Emma nods, and looks at me with a smile that combines surprise, respect, and affection. "Gosh," she says. "You're different, Sophie. How'd you get to be so sure of yourself all of a sudden?"

"Oh," I say with a secret smile. "A friend helped me."

The End

To read this story another way and see how different choices lead to a different ending, turn back to page 11.

ABOUT Maryellen's Time

In many ways, the 1950s were a good time to grow up. As Sophie observes, kids had more free time and fewer scheduled activities than many children today. They roamed freely in their neighborhoods, biking and walking to local parks, stores, and even the beach on their own. If a parent was needed, their mothers were usually at home.

Staying at home to raise a family was presented as the proper goal in life for girls and women. Popular TV shows like *Father Knows Best* and *Leave It to Beaver* portrayed the "ideal" family, with the father employed outside the home and the mother as a homemaker focused on caring for her family. In reality, one third of women worked—as teachers, nurses, secretaries, waitresses, and many other jobs—but employers often expected a woman to leave her job when she got married or started a family. So it was hard for women in the 1950s to build careers and to support themselves and their families financially the way they can today.

Some homemakers found creative ways to earn money on the side. *Jingles*, or songs and verses that advertise a product, were very popular in the 1950s. Businesses sometimes held contests and invited the public to submit slogans and jingles for their products, much like the contest that Maryellen enters in the story. The rhyming Burma Shave signs were so popular and successful that the company held an annual contest, paying $100 for any verse it used. One woman named Evelyn Ryan helped support her ten children by entering jingle contests for Burma Shave and other brands. Her slogans and verses were so clever that she often won prizes—including cash, groceries, trips, appliances, a case of candy bars, and a car!

While some women were happy to focus on home and family, others wanted to pursue other subjects that interested them. One of the less positive aspects about the 1950s is that traditionally male professions like science were all but closed to women. Accustomed to seeing only male doctors, lawyers, professors, and scientists, many people thought that women couldn't do those jobs—that "girls can't be scientists," as Nancy's brother tells her in the story.

Slowly but surely, women began proving that they *could* do those jobs. Botanist and genetics pioneer Barbara McClintock showed how genes control physical characteristics, but her male colleagues dismissed her research. Later, her theories were proven right, and she won the Nobel Prize in 1983. Other leading scientists from Maryellen's time include Dian Fossey, famous for her research on mountain gorillas; Rachel Carson, whose books launched the environmental movement; and Vera Rubin, who discovered that galaxies are clustered, rather than evenly sprinkled, throughout the universe. By persevering and overcoming the prevailing view that science was for men, these women and many others paved the way for girls like Nancy, Sophie, and Maryellen, and inspired them to become archaeologists, astronomers, writers, artists, and anything else they dreamed of being.

Read more of MARYELLEN'S stories,

available from booksellers and at *americangirl.com*

✳ *Classics* ✳

Maryellen's classic series, now in two volumes:

Volume 1:
The One and Only

Maryellen wants to stand out—but when she draws a cartoon of her teacher, she also draws unwanted attention. Still, her drawing skills help her make a new friend—with a girl her old friends think of as an enemy!

Volume 2:
Taking Off

Maryellen's birthday party is a huge hit! Excited by her fame, she enters a science contest. But can Maryellen invent a flying machine *and* get her sister's wedding off the ground?

✳ *Journey in Time* ✳

Travel back in time—and spend a few days with Maryellen!

The Sky's the Limit

Step into Maryellen's world of the 1950s! Go to a sock hop, or take a road trip with the Larkin family all the way to Washington, D.C. Choose your own path through this multiple-ending story.

A Sneak Peek at

The One
and Only

A Maryellen Classic

What happens to Maryellen?
Find out in the first volume of her classic stories.

aryellen Larkin liked to make up episodes of her favorite TV shows and imagine herself in them. This morning, for example, as she was walking down the hot, sunny sidewalk with her dog, Scooter, to mail a letter to her grandparents, she was pretending that she was in an episode of *The Lone Ranger*. Her only companion was her trusty horse, Thunderbolt. (That was Scooter's part.) Maryellen leaned forward as if she were battling her way through a blinding blizzard. If she didn't deliver the medicine in her hand, hundreds of people would die.

Maryellen never gave herself superpowers in any of her imagined shows. She didn't fly or do magic or become invisible or anything. She looked the way she really looked, except maybe a little taller and with better clothes. The main difference was that in her TV shows, everyone paid attention to her. They listened to her great ideas, they followed her advice, and—*ta-da!*—everything turned out just right.

Maryellen ceremoniously put her letter in the mailbox, imagining that she was handing medicine to a kindly old doctor in the snowy town in the Old West. "Thank you, Miss Larkin, ma'am," the imaginary

doctor said. "We desperately needed this. You have saved hundreds of lives today."

Maryellen smiled modestly and shrugged as if to say, "It was nothing." Then she turned to go. "Come on, Thunderbolt," she said to Scooter. "Our work is done."

Scooter, a stout and elderly dachshund, had *just* flopped down and made himself comfortable in the shade of the mailbox. But Maryellen whispered, "Come on, Scooter. Get up, old boy." So Scooter rose with a good-natured sigh and waddled behind Maryellen, who pretended to trudge through drifts of snow as grateful townspeople called after her, "Thank you, Miss Larkin! You're our hero!"

"Hey, Ellie," said a real voice, calling her by her nickname. The voice belonged to her friend Davy Fenstermacher, who lived next door in a house that looked exactly like the Larkins' house. Maryellen and Davy had been friends forever.

"Howdy, pardner," Maryellen drawled.

"I'll race you to the swing!" said Davy. "On your mark, get set, *go*!"

Maryellen and Davy ran to the Larkins' backyard, with Scooter loping along behind them. Maryellen got to the swing first, jumped on, and began to pump. "I win!" she called down to Davy. "You be the Lone Ranger, stuck in quicksand, and I'll jump down and rescue you."

"Okay," said Davy agreeably. Of course, they both knew that cowboys didn't usually jump off swings. But the swing that Mr. Larkin had hung in the backyard was so much fun that they used it in lots of the TV shows they made up.

Maryellen swung high and then jumped off. "Ya*hoo*!" she hollered, swooping through the August air. She landed on the grass with a soft thud. "Come on, Thunderbolt!" she called to Scooter. "We've got to save the Lone Ranger!"

Scooter, asleep in the shade, snored.

"Better wake him up first, Ellie," said Davy.

But before Maryellen could rouse Scooter, her six-year-old sister, Beverly, came clomping out of the house in an old pair of Mrs. Larkin's high heels. Beverly wore one of Dad's baseball caps turned inside out so that it looked like a crown. She also wore three pop-bead necklaces and two pop-bead bracelets, one on each arm. Right behind Beverly came Tom and

Mikey, Maryellen's younger brothers.

"What are you doing?" Beverly asked.

"Nothing," said Maryellen, wishing that Beverly and the boys would go back inside, but knowing that they wouldn't. Maryellen, Beverly, Tom, and Mikey shared a bedroom, and even though the little kids were cute and sweet and goofy, they drove Maryellen crazy, especially the boys. One time, while she was at school, the boys got into her *I Love Lucy* paper dolls and she found Lucy's clothes scattered all over the floor like confetti and Lucy folded up in one of Tom's toy trucks. Lucy had never been able to hold her head up again. Now that it was summer, Beverly, Tom, and Mikey stuck to her like glue, twenty-four hours a day. They couldn't bear to be left out of anything fun that she might be doing.

Sure enough, Beverly said, "I want to play with you and Davy!"

"Me too!" said Tom.

"Me!" said Mikey.

Davy shot Maryellen a sympathetic look. He had years of experience dealing with Beverly, Tom, and Mikey.

Thinking quickly, Maryellen suggested to Davy, "What if the little kids are in the quicksand, too, and I rescue all of you?"

"Good idea," said Davy.

"Pretend I'm a queen that you're rescuing," said Beverly.

"Oh, brother," Maryellen muttered. That was another problem with Beverly. She liked to pretend, but she always pretended the same thing: that she was a queen. Dad called her Queen Beverly. "I don't think they had queens in the Wild West," Maryellen said. "I've never seen one on a TV show, anyway. Have you, Davy?"

"Nope," said Davy firmly.

Maryellen smiled. Good old Davy always backed her up. She said to Beverly, clinching the point, "And Davy and I have watched almost every TV show there ever was."

Queen Beverly looked stubborn. Maryellen was just about to give in to Her Majesty when their mother called out the back door, "Ellie, honey, come in for a minute. I need you."

"Okay," called Maryellen, feeling pleased. Mom needed *her*!

Maryellen's pride wilted just a bit when Mom added, "Beverly, Tom, and Mikey, you come, too." She wished Mom wouldn't always lump her together with Beverly, Tom, and Mikey as if they were one big bumpy creature with four heads, eight arms, and eight legs. Mom certainly treated Maryellen's older sisters, Joan and Carolyn, as separate, serious people.

I'm tired of being one of the "little kids," grumped Maryellen to herself, for the millionth time. *I guess I'm stuck with Beverly, but I'm much too grown-up to share a room with Tom and Mikey. Somehow, I have to convince Mom that I should share a bedroom with Joan and Carolyn so that she'll think of me as one of the "big girls" and take me— and my ideas—more seriously.*

"Come on, kids," said Mom. She scooped Mikey up onto her hip and held out her free hand to Tom. Beverly clomped along as quickly as she could in her high heels. Scooter rose stiffly and followed her.

"What do you need us for, Mom?" asked Maryellen.

"Just a quick family meeting," said Mom.

"Oh," said Maryellen without enthusiasm. She knew from experience that it was hard to get a word in edgewise during family meetings. They were not at

all like one of her pretend TV shows where she was the hero and everyone hung on her every word. Maryellen sighed and said to Davy, "See you later, alligator."

"In a while, crocodile," said Davy. "I'll wait here."

Maryellen walked into the kitchen and slid onto the bench in the breakfast nook next to Joan, her eldest sister. Joan, who was seventeen and therefore nearly all grown up, looked sideways at Maryellen's grass-stained shorts and inched away, closer to Carolyn. It was crowded on the bench, but Maryellen wanted Mom to see her next to Joan and Carolyn, on their side of the table, so that Mom would think of the three of them as a group. Maryellen could tell that this family meeting would be like all the others: frustrating. The kitchen was already noisy. Dad had left on a three-day business trip earlier that morning, but Mom and Carolyn, Maryellen's next-oldest sister, were talking a mile a minute. Tom was wailing like a siren as he rode his toy fire truck around the kitchen. Mikey was yodeling and banging a spoon on the tray connected to his high chair. Mrs. Larkin took Mikey's spoon away from him and gave him a piece of toast, which was quieter to bang, and then said, "Kids!"

Everyone quieted down.

"I have an important announcement," said Mrs. Larkin. "My friends Betty and Florence are coming to spend the night."

"Who're Fletty and Borence?" asked Beverly.

"*B*etty and *F*lorence," said Mrs. Larkin. "You kids have never met them. We worked together at the factory. They live in New York City now. We're going to a reunion luncheon at the factory tomorrow." Maryellen knew that Mom was referring to the aircraft factory where she had worked during World War Two.

"I'm glad Betty and Florence are coming," said Maryellen. Her mind sped ahead. Lots of TV quiz shows were filmed in New York City. Maybe Mom's friends could get her a spot on one of them! She'd be the youngest contestant *ever*—

Joan interrupted Maryellen's daydream with a practical question. "Where will Betty and Florence sleep?" she asked Mom.

Maryellen's mind sped ahead again. This could be the moment she had been waiting for all summer! "I have an idea," she announced.

About the Author

VALERIE TRIPP says that she became a writer because of the kind of person she is. She says she's curious, and writing requires you to be interested in everything. Talking is her favorite sport, and writing is a way of talking on paper. She's a daydreamer, which helps her come up with her ideas. And she loves words. She even loves the struggle to come up with just the right words as she writes and rewrites. Ms. Tripp lives in Maryland with her husband.